D1282967

Pointing the Way

AMS PRESS
NEW YORK

Pointing the Way

BY

SUTTON E. GRIGGS

NASHVILLE, TENN.
THE ORION PUBLISHING COMPANY
1908

Library of Congress Cataloging in Publication Data

Griggs, Sutton Elbert, 1872-
Pointing the way.

I. Title.
PZ3.G888Po9 [PS3513.R7154] 813'.5'2 75-144622
ISBN 0-404-00167-X

Reprinted from the edition of 1908, Nashville
First AMS edition published, 1974
Manufactured in the United States of America

AMS PRESS, INC.
New York, N.Y. 10003

DEDICATION.

AFFECTIONATELY DEDICATED TO

MY WIFE,

IN THE HOPE THAT SHE MAY FIND HEREIN SOMEWHAT OF AN EXPLANATION OF THAT OCCASIONAL FAR-AWAY LOOK IN THE EYES, OF WHICH, IN HER WIFELY SOLICITUDE, SHE HAS FROM TIME TO TIME QUITE PROPERLY MADE COMPLAINT.

THE AUTHOR.

CONTENTS.

CHAPTER I. PAGE.
A Face of Mystery ... 7
CHAPTER II.
A Puzzled Lawyer ... 18
CHAPTER III.
Objections to a Marriage ... 29
CHAPTER IV.
The Visit Is Made ... 35
CHAPTER V.
Yet Debating ... 44
CHAPTER VI.
She Investigates ... 54
CHAPTER VII.
The Parson Flees ... 61
CHAPTER VIII.
Uncle Jack's Conversion ... 69
CHAPTER IX.
The Man Appears ... 74
CHAPTER X.
Conroe Driscoll ... 79
CHAPTER XI.
Eina Begins to Plan ... 87
CHAPTER XII.
That Is the Question ... 95
CHAPTER XIII.
Eina and Baug ... 100
CHAPTER XIV.
A Strange Letter ... 104
CHAPTER XV.
She Insists ... 111
CHAPTER XVI.
The Crux ... 116
CHAPTER XVII.
Molair on the Alert ... 125
CHAPTER XVIII.
Kicked Out ... 132

CHAPTER XIX. PAGE.
Tight Place for Uncle Jack 138
CHAPTER XX.
Funeral of a Live Man 146
CHAPTER XXI.
The Break 151
CHAPTER XXII.
Light Comes 158
CHAPTER XXIII.
Quite Unexpected 163
CHAPTER XXIV.
Baug Searching for Eina 166
CHAPTER XXV.
Clear Sailing 174
CHAPTER XXVI.
Desires Her Will Changed 178
CHAPTER XXVII.
Molair at Work 184
CHAPTER XXVIII.
The North and the South 190
CHAPTER XXIX.
Molair and an Old Friend 194
CHAPTER XXX.
The Rudolf Fire 200
CHAPTER XXXI.
A Fortune Spurned 204
CHAPTER XXXII.
A Badly Needed Opening 207
CHAPTER XXXIII.
Sunshine and Storm 212
CHAPTER XXXIV.
A Chinese Lady 220
CHAPTER XXXV.
A Frightened Justice 224
CHAPTER XXXVI.
Disfranchisement Forgotten 229

CHAPTER I.

A FACE OF MYSTERY.

"WHY, dear, what on earth—"

The question thus begun was never finished. As to why the questioner felt impelled to begin the query only to drop it unceremoniously in its unfinished state it will presently appear.

It was midday, and a midsummer sun of the Southern skies was beating down fiercely upon that loveliest of all Southern cities, Belrose, the very mention of whose name recalls to those who have seen it, visions of a cleanly, hustling business center, well-regulated streets, beautiful but not ostentatious suburban homes, an amplitude of trees with rich green foliage, rows of magnolias, testifying by leaf and flower to the exuberance of the gifts of soil and air; recalls that air of serenity that pervades the city at eventide as the hum of business grows less, as night begins to deftly weave her robe of gloom, as the glare of the electric lights comes forth to aid a shirking moon and the timid stars.

But we must get back to the hot, sultry day, and not be tempted from our recital by the physical charms of the city of Belrose. The extreme heat of the day was indicated by swiftly moving fans and upraised parasols in the hands of the lady pedestrians on the streets, by the holding of hats in their hands and coats on their arms on the part of the men, and by the almost religious zeal with which shady spots were sought by those whose missions called upon them to wait.

On the faces of all there was a half-encouraged, half-resisted look of worriment. One fat, rotund man, rather low of stature, came toddling along, his collar and his handkerchief drenched with perspiration, while his good nature made a last grand stand against the efforts of the atmosphere to vex him beyond measure. To a leaner companion walking by his side he said:

"By gosh, Jim, this is about the best time I'll get, don't you think?"

"For what?" asked his companion.

"For croaking. I guess it's all settled where a rounder like me is to go when he pegs out. I was just thinking that if I could drop out of Belrose to-day and land at once in His Satanic Majesty's big kitchen, the change of atmosphere would not be so violent as to upset my delicate system. See?"

Among the vehicles passing along Broadway was a phaeton occupied by two young women, one of them being closely veiled; the other was driving. Suddenly the young lady who was driving lowered the phaeton top and thus invited a more direct contact with the rays of the zealous sun.

The lady with the veil had just arrived in Belrose from more northerly regions, and the heat, oppressive to the native Belrosans, was doubly so to her. Imagine, therefore, her surprise at the seemingly purposeless lowering of the phaeton top, which act on the part of her friend begot the unfinished query to which we have just listened. But, as we have said, the question was not finished, for at that instant the eye of the veiled lady wandered to the near street corner to the left, just ahead of them, and something there seemed to arouse in her a sharp, deep interest. Abandoning the unfinished question the veiled lady propounded another.

Looking straight ahead, she said quickly: "Clotille, be circumspect about it, but let the horse walk slowly, and look at that man standing on the near corner to your left. Who is he?"

Clotille did as directed, and said: "To be sure, I see several men on the corner, Eina."

"Oh, I mean *the* man, the man with his hat in one hand and a handkerchief in the other."

Clotille cautiously stole a second glance in the direction indicated. A merry laugh with an undercurrent of satisfaction that did not escape Eina's acute ear, and which in later days she so vividly recalled, came from Clotille, somewhat to Eina's confusion.

"Now, Clotille, at what are you laughing? Is the gent in question Belrose's all-conquering gallant? And do you think that I have fallen a victim to his charms and—at sight, too? Why, Clotille Strange!" said Eina, in loving, reproachful tones.

"Oh, be fair to me, Eina. Cannot your friend, Clotille, indulge in a tiny laugh when Eina of the cold heart (when it comes to the sterner sex) happens to see a strange, handsome young man, and takes so much as even a passing interest in him? Is it not time for me to sit up and take notice?"

"Eina changeth not, Clotille."

"My dear, dear girl, I do not misjudge you. I know only too well of the steel casing about your heart," said Clotille, dropping her playful tone.

"Well, back to that little laugh of yours, Clotille. Why did you laugh when I made my inquiry concerning the man with his hat in his hand? There was something behind that laugh, Clotille."

"Let us take up things in their order, Eina. We will come to the smile by and by, but let us first deal with the man."

"All right, the man, then," rejoined Eina.

"The man's name is Baug Peppers."

"Why, *Clotille!*" exclaimed Eina, almost rising from the buggy seat. "You *must* be mistaken. No being with a head, and face, and eyes such as that man has could *ever* have so unpoetic a name. Baug! Peppers! It is simply ridiculous," said Eina, with evident warmth, her sense of the eternal fitness of things being grievously outraged.

"Well, that is his name, just the same," said Clotille.

"Clotille, *you* may think so, *he* may think so, but as assuredly as your name is Clotille Strange, that man's real name is not Baug Peppers. I *know* it is not."

"Well, we will waive that question for the time being. Now that you know what his name is at least *said* to be, what have you further to say?" asked Clotille.

"His mind has certainly written itself on his face. He is brainy and true. One can see that at a glance. It seems to me that I have seen him before," said Eina.

"When? Where?" asked Clotille.

"I don't just recall," said Eina.

"I will give you a few moments in which to recall just when and where you met him, and will not disturb you with my chatter while you reflect," said Clotille.

Eina now leaned back in the phaeton and gave herself up to an earnest effort to recall just when, where, and under what circumstances she had seen this Mr. Baug Peppers before. The thing that puzzled her most was that Mr. Peppers was a man of such a striking personal appearance that people generally would be supposed to have no difficulty in recalling having seen or met him, but here she was, almost positive that she had seen him before, and yet utterly unable to in any manner trace the impression.

By and by Eina said: "Clotille, I give it up. Every now and then it seems as though my mind is upon the point of grasping the solution as to his face, whereupon it nimbly slips by and eludes me."

"Now, I will explain my smile," said Clotille.

"The impression created by that man's face is Belrose's standing mystery, and is a most unique phenomenon. To begin with, the face seems to impress every one. We Belrosans all like to look at it, it matters not how often we have seen it. Visitors invariably pay special attention to it, and it always arouses the thought in them that they have seen it before or some face that greatly resembles it. But we have yet to find the person who has stated that he has satisfied his own consciousness as to the identity of the other face suggested by this face. So there comes into the minds of strangers and there lives in our minds a suggested personality that ever remains nameless."

"How very, very queer," said Eina, quietly, still trying to condense the nebulous thought that had been sent floating through her mind by the face.

"At times," continued Clotille, "we have had conventions of national scope to assemble here, and have entertained groups of delegates at social gatherings; and it was at one time a source of much amusement to us to have our guests one after another go through the same series of questions and answers that you and I in the first instance indulged in to-day with regard to that face until the matter became so tiresome to Baug that he began to avoid all social gatherings at which strangers were likely to be present."

"He knows, then, of the peculiar impression made by his face," remarked Eina.

"Oh, yes, and he has gotten so that, when introduced, he quietly remarks before the stranger gets an opportunity to make the stereotyped comment which he knows is forthcoming, 'Of course you think you have seen me before, or think you have seen someone that looks like me, but for the life of you, you can't tell where you saw me nor who it is that I resemble, so let us pass all that by,'" said Clotille.

"Decidedly interesting, and I, Eina Rapona, am going to try to find an answer to the puzzle. Somehow I feel that something great, something tremendous lies behind this Belrose phenomenon. I am not a prophetess, nor the seventh daughter of a seventh daughter, but I venture the prediction that I shall furnish an explanation of this phenomenon, and that, upon discovery, it will excite more interest than it does as a mystery. Mark my words, I feel it. I know not why. I am not a sentimentalist at all, but there is something great betokened by that man's face and some tremendous fact lies behind it," Eina remarked.

Had Eina been observing Clotille's face closely she ought to have been able to see that this resolve on her part was for some reason giving Clotille a deep measure of satisfaction.

"Well, I must explain another little matter to you," said Clotille. "Mr. Peppers has solemnly vowed that he will wed the girl that unravels this mystery. Now, will you permit me to smile to my heart's content, since you, the queen of the anti-marriage brigade, have so diligently resolved upon earning your title to a husband?" asked Clotille, laughingly.

"Dear me! Forewarned is forearmed. *That* is a game in which at least two have a say. You don't balk me, Clotille. I must solve this riddle, just the same, do you hear?"

"Well, Eina, you are welcome to your task, but as to how you are going to even start about this matter I don't know. If you succeed, I shall crown you queen of detectives."

"Oh, say," added Clotille, "Mr. Peppers in former days took a deep interest in some phases of politics, and once formed part of a delegation that called upon a President of the United States. And, don't you know, even the President singled him out and made the usual remarks to him. After all, as you say, there may be something back of such a universal conception."

"Indeed! Indeed! I simply must know why it is that I feel within that I have seen this man before. I simply must," said Eina.

At last Clotille and Eina reached the cottage where the latter was to dwell. There it sat crowning a hill, far out on the outskirts of Belrose, commanding a splendid view of the city and of all the surrounding territory. As Eina entered the cottage yard she was thrilled with the beauty of the scene before her.

"Oh, Clotille, you are a born artist. Just look at that rich green grass; at the lovely arrangement of the rose bushes; at the star-shaped beds from which those tiny flowers, of every tint and hue, peep at one so sweetly! Look at those pretty ferns. They haven't the petals of the flowers, but they seem to know their beauty and are careful to display it."

Lifting her eyes to the beautifully shaped cottage, she gazed at the profusion of honeysuckles that clambered over and fully covered the cottage walls.

"Oh, I share with you your love of the snug cottage, you dear clinging honeysuckles. It would seem to me that if I were dead and should pass this way, this beautiful spot would awaken my soul and call me back to life again," said Eina, her bosom heaving with the delight that surged up from her heart.

Tears of joy stood in Clotille's eyes, for upon her had fallen the whole task of choosing and arranging this home for her wealthy friend, and she was therefore highly gratified that her friend seemed so well pleased.

As they stood making a survey of the place, the Negro servant, a tall, aged man, came walking around the house. He had an erect, soldierly carriage, which was somewhat modified by the humble carrying of his hat in his hand and the deferential inclining of his head slightly forward, a combination of dignity and humility. His mustache, beard and hair were white, and his solemn face thus enveloped would have been a little awesome but for the kindly light that gleamed in his eyes.

Clotille whispered to Eina, saying, "That old man is as honest as a monk, as solemn as an owl, and as keen a lover of the humorous as you ever saw."

"Indeed! He does not look it," said Eina.

When the servant had approached as near as an attitude of profound deference would permit, Clotille said, "Uncle Jack, this is Miss Eina Rapona, who is to be your landlady."

Uncle Jack bowed low, and a look of pleasure came into his black face. He was very sensitive on the point as to the class of people he was to serve, and was a keen judge of what he called "quality folks." This pleased look was due to the fact that Eina had stood the test of his keen intuition.

Clotille, who had secured Uncle Jack to serve Eina, eyed him closely, and was delighted at the signals of pleasure that her friend had caused to appear in the countenance of this veteran Negro connoisseur of faces.

It was very vital to Clotille's plans that Eina should please Uncle Jack, for in the schemes that she had before her she had need of him.

When Clotille had escorted Eina into the house and had gone from room to room, showing how she had fitted it up for Eina's comfort, she then left her friend and drove back toward Belrose, a smile of happiness on her lips, the light of joy in her eyes.

"Well, sir, it worked like a charm. It worked like a charm." Such was the happy reflection that came and came again to, or, speaking more accurately, that abode in, Clotille's mind.

CHAPTER II.

A PUZZLED LAWYER.

THROUGHOUT the somewhat restless night which Eina spent in her new home, whether waking or sleeping, the face of Baug Peppers, the face of mystery, with its elusive suggestiveness, haunted her. When, on the morning following, Eina arose to greet the new day, and threw open her blinds to let in the cheering light of the sun, this face of mystery was still the uninvited but persistent guest of her mind. Could Clotille but have known just how much Eina's thoughts were occupied with this new, strange face that had suddenly thrust itself across the pathway of her life, she would perhaps have felt inclined to regard it as a stroke of genius on her part to have hit upon such a successful plan for the furtherance of her purposes.

Incident to Eina's making Belrose her home, there were some business matters that had to be adjusted, and Clotille had arranged for Eina to call that morning at the office of one Seth Molair. When, therefore, the dainty breakfast prepared by Uncle Jack was over, Eina repaired to her room to attire herself for that business call. Of course Eina would not have admitted it, would have denied it to her own consciousness, but it is nevertheless true that the possibility that she might meet the man with the mysterious face influenced her in the matter of her toilet.

From her earliest youth the world had taken pains to inform Eina over and over again as to how beautiful she was, but hitherto she had been rather indifferent to the fact of nature's rich endowment, and none ever thought to call her vain.

But as she now stood before her mirror taking an inventory of what might be termed her charms, there was in her eyes, in this privacy of her dressing room, the plainest sort of hungering for the beautiful in herself.

"Has the world judged aright? Am I beautiful?" asked Eina of herself. She lifted her bared, rounded arms, tapering so exquisitely at the wrists, and gazed at them for a few seconds, then lowered them. Eina now turned her attention to her face, neither oval nor long, perfectly proportioned, her features—mouth, nose, ears, forehead—each a work of art in itself. And well did her wealth of hair, black at a distance, but brown at close range, grace her head. And well might her eyes, those wondrously expressive, beautiful black eyes, matching well the long, dark brown eyelashes and heavy eyebrows—well might her eyes, the dominating center of a realm of beauty, gleam with that subtle, inexplicable charm that made a friend of every one who gazed into their soulful depths.

Gifted with a rare taste in choosing and blending those colors which best suited and accentuated her beauty, Eina, when ready for her trip into the city, was beyond all cavil a vision of loveliness.

"It is one uv my rights, miss, ter 'spress myself 'bout de looks uv de lady folks uv my famblys whar I wuks. I doan' wuk fur none but quality folks. Yer air de puttiest lady I evah wukked fur," said Uncle Jack, with a paternal pride in Eina's appearance, as he drove her to the city.

Bubbling over with good humor, Uncle Jack talked to Eina as they rode along, giving her scraps of history of Belrose.

When Eina arrived at Seth Molair's office, instead of being at once ushered into his presence, as was to have been expected in view of the character of the business engagement that she had with him, she was kept waiting in the ante-room for some considerable time.

In the office in which Eina sat there was a large, magnificent mirror. Seth Molair, the occupant of the suite of rooms, desiring to have an opportunity to study clients unobserved by them, so arranged the chairs in his waiting-room that this mirror recorded likenesses at such an angle that he could, by the use of a strong opera glass, constructed in the partition between the two offices, get a splendid view of people without their suspecting that he was observing them.

The explanation of Molair's prolonged delay in admitting Eina was that he was both charmed and puzzled. Eina, as we have seen, had taken special pains with her toilet, and Molair was struck with the amazing beauty of the girl, who impressed him as being undoubtedly the most beautiful woman upon whom his eyes had ever fallen. He was sorely puzzled, too, as to Eina's nationality, a consideration which, in Belrose, as in all Southern cities, counted for a great deal.

Eina's complexion had been the bane of many an artist's life, portrait painters having despaired of reproducing its beautiful tints, defying, as they did, the power of the brush and pen. She was light enough of complexion to pass among the whites for a white girl, had just enough of the dark in her complexion to permit her to pass as a colored woman if she so elected, while the underglow of red in her complexion, coupled with her beautiful black eyes and the appearance of her hair, suggested that Indian blood was not altogether missing from her veins.

"Of whatever nationality, it would seem that the races of mankind have united to make this girl the composite beauty of the human family," reflected Molair.

At length Molair opened the door of his private office and bade Eina to enter. After a formal introduction, the two settled down to the business on hand. Seth Molair was noted for his dispatch in business matters, but it must be confessed that in this particular instance he did not live up to his reputation. He did not overly prolong the interview, but simply proceeded with marked deliberation, regarding it as a genuine treat to have the privilege to merely contemplate the exquisite beauty of the face before him.

The question of Eina's nationality continued to give Molair concern. There were, to be sure, the European features and the stamp of European culture and spirit, but there was that faint, picturesque tinge of the dark that might or might not be due to a distant connection with the land that chose to make sable her sons and daughters. Molair resolved to discover Eina's racial affiliation before the interview was over, and began to manœuver to attain that end. He had been told that in every light person having a vestige of Negro blood in their veins there was a slight muddiness behind their ears. Pretending to have business across the room to the rear of Eina, Molair managed to get behind her and to glance at her ears.

"No special mark there," was his mental note as he gazed upon Eina's pretty neck and ears.

Molair had heard that at the roots of the finger nails there was always to be found a telltale sign that betrayed the presence of Negro blood when all other indications failed, but Eina had on gloves, which prevented a resort to that test. However, Molair decided to overcome this obstacle. Excusing himself rather abruptly, he entered his outer office, closed the door, and had the white girl who was his stenographer to come to him at the office window, where he took a look at the roots of her finger nails and at his own. Having familiarized himself with the appearance of the finger nails of himself and his stenographer, he re-entered the office to plan for testing Eina.

When the time came for Eina to sign the papers incident to their business transaction, Molair had her take a seat at a small table in the center of the room, the table being just large enough to hold the papers to be signed, but not large enough for the inkstand in addition thereto. Molair stood near her, holding the inkstand in his hand, and leaned over ostensibly to point out just where she was to sign. In so doing, in keeping with his plan, he spilled the ink upon Eina's glove.

"Clumsy! Clumsy! Clumsy! I beg a thousand pardons," said Molair.

Eina looked up, her mind in perfect accord with Molair's suggestion that he was clumsy. She gave him a reassuring smile, however, to drive away his embarrassment, and said, "I should have taken off my gloves to write, anyway, so the fault is mine, not yours."

"That is quite generous in you, Miss Rapona, but I do not pardon myself. Miss Grainger," called Molair, to his stenographer, who now entered, "Take that glove off of Miss Rapona's hand, step across the street to the store, and bring us another pair."

Miss Grainger approached to draw off the glove and Molair, at the risk of being thought rude, stood so as to be able to see the finger nails as the glove left the hand. In his conference with his stenographer he had told her of his plan, and had asked her to be as deliberate as possible in getting the glove off of the finger tips, that he might have as good an opportunity as possible to see the finger nails. Slowly the glove came off, Molair's eager eyes following every inch of its progress. When at last the finger nails stood revealed, and Molair's keen gaze was directed towards them, he heaved a sigh of relief and said, "Heaven be praised!" The finger nail roots were normal.

Eina looked at Molair inquiringly, unable to account for his exclamation. Molair caught the meaning of the look, but proffered no explanation. When the papers had all been signed, Molair broached the question that had been uppermost in his mind, feeling free to do so, since Miss Rapona was able by any test to be classified as white.

"Miss Rapona," began he, "the white people of the South are not individualists. With the possibility of racial antagonisms on the one hand and social commingling on the other always confronting us, we are more or less in a chronic state of spiritual war, and, just as in time of war you do not allow the individual soldiers personal liberty, we withhold a great measure of personal liberty from all Southern people, white and colored, and maintain certain well-defined customs."

Eina became all interest and waited breathlessly Molair's deliverances.

"You are from Boston, where social freedom—the thing that people are trying to say when they say social equality—exists. In the South social freedom is not permitted, for reasons that I need not discuss just here. Whoever affiliates socially with the one race in the South is denied the social life of the other. Will you regard it as a piece of impertinence on my part to ask you as to where you are to cast your lot socially?"

"You mean to say that there is no such thing as being allowed to treat all upon the score of individual merit?" remarked Eina.

"Exactly. Choice, in the South, lies not between individuals, but between races. Moreover, if you have once passed as a white person, you will not be allowed to drop into the colored race. On the other hand, if you are once classed as a colored person, you can never change to the white race where that fact is known," replied Molair.

"Would you white people of the South accept me?" asked Eina.

"Pardon me, but what is your blood?" asked Molair.

"I am of English, Spanish and Indian descent. Of course you know that the Spaniards drew the dark in their complexion from the Moors, who of course are Africans. By both my Spanish and Indian blood, which, however, is all but lost in the English strain, I am connected with the colored races of the world."

"Now let us see," said Molair. "We of the

South place no ban upon intermarriage with the Spanish people. The glorious history of Spain has baptized her slight swarthiness, and we forget the Moor. As for the Indians, our President has advised their absorption into our blood. According to prevailing standards you would find no barrier to your entrance into the white race.

"On the other hand, there is the tinge of the dark in your complexion which will permit you to classify yourself as colored if you so desire. There are hundreds of people right here in Belrose even lighter than you are, lighter than thousands of whites, who are classed as colored."

"I find myself, therefore, in the unique position of being allowed to choose for myself my racial home. For most people that is a thing entirely beyond their control," said Eina, smiling sadly.

"Before you make your choice, Miss Rapona, would you kindly allow me to canvass the whole situation with you?" asked Molair, speaking with evident earnestness.

"I know of nothing that would give me greater pleasure, Mr. Molair," said Eina, much pleased at a prospective arrangement that would give her a glance into the heart of the South, that willy-nilly had written itself into her Boston's daily thought and nightly dream.

Molair paused awhile, hesitating as to whether to say what he had in mind, and searching for the best form in which to put what he would like to say.

Noting his embarrassment, Eina said, "Feel free, Mr. Molair, to speak your mind to me."

"I could, Miss Rapona, discuss these matters with you here, but somehow, when the deeper issues of life are involved, I like to get away from this office, be free from its atmosphere altogether. Here, in an honorable way, I hope, I look after my personal interests by trying to faithfully serve my clients. Elsewhere I am an unfettered man, the human being."

"Why can you not come to my home?" asked Eina.

"There is the rub. For the present at least you wish to keep the question of your social alignment open. It is well known in Belrose that I make no professional visits. My clients all come to me. If I call to see you it will be surmised that I call to see you socially, and if it became known to the colored people that I so visit you, you can never thereafter reach their best social life, perhaps," said Molair.

"Why cannot I call at your home, then?" asked Eina.

"If you enter my home as a social visitor to my mother, you take rank as a white person. If you once assume rank as a white person, you can never in the South drop into the life of the colored people unless you can show clear title to Negro blood. We don't allow it," said Molair.

"Who stays with you at your home, Miss Rapona?" asked Molair.

"One Jack Morris; Uncle Jack they call him," replied Eina.

"Uncle Jack! Why, I know Uncle Jack, and a truer soul never lived," said Molair.

"I was about to suggest, Mr. Molair, that Uncle Jack might bring you to my home unobserved. I feel that it means so much to be permitted to hear what you have to say," said Eina.

"That is about the only way in which all objections can be met," said Molair.

So it was agreed that, under the chaperonage of Uncle Jack, Molair was to clandestinely visit Eina.

"By the way, is the man with the face of mystery a colored man or a white man? I did not think to ask Clotille," mused Eina, as, sitting by the side of Uncle Jack, she journeyed back to her home out from Belrose.

CHAPTER III.

OBJECTIONS TO A MARRIAGE.

BEFORE Molair pays the promised visit to Eina with a view to influencing her social alignment, it is perhaps expedient that we learn something of the influences that brought her to Belrose, something of the situation, to play a vital part in which she had come, so that, as we stand with her in the momentous hour of her choice of race we may be the better prepared to sit in judgment on her course.

In order that we may get into this position of vantage, it is necessary for us to go back and catch up a thread that by and by merges into the situation presented at the point where this drama of human life first unfolds itself to your view.

In the days of slavery two Negro sisters, with the doings, more or less, of whose descendants we shall have to deal, were assigned diverse destinies, the one of them choosing a mate within the Negro race and becoming the maternal antecedent of a line of people of dark complexion, while the other became the maternal founder of a line of people of mixed blood.

When freedom came, Constantine Gilbreath, the white man involved in the alignment mentioned, did not abandon nor suffer to depart the Negro woman whose companion he had been in slavery, but continued the relationship.

Among their children was Letitia Gilbreath, who was born to them a few years after the close of the civil war. Upon the death of Constantine Gilbreath, his fortune, which was considerable, was apportioned among the members of his Negro family. Letitia Gilbreath inherited from her father a marked commercial talent and love of gain, which faculty she devoted to the increase of the holdings bequeathed to her, and as a result grew to be a fairly wealthy woman, as wealth went in the Southland.

Miss Letitia declined all offers of matrimony, grew to be regarded as an eccentric old maid, devoted her entire thought to her possessions, and seemed to shut out from her heart all her fellow-men and women with two exceptions, as follows: A daughter of her mother's sister married and became the mother of a beautiful dark girl whose pretty face and black appealing eyes had somehow reached the soft spot in Miss Letitia's heart. She applied to her cousin, Mrs. Hannah Strange, for this beautiful dark child, Clotille, reared and educated it. She had resolved, should the girl marry in a manner that pleased her, to make a bridal present of one-half of her fortune, and to provide in her will that Clotille should come into possession of the other half upon the testator's death. Miss Letitia's fancy had likewise gone out for Baug Peppers, as a boy, and she had resolved upon him as a husband for Clotille, the fact that Baug was very light of complexion counting greatly in his favor, this in truth being a determining consideration.

Miss Letitia, herself a mulatto, would have denied most vehemently that she was at all prejudiced as to color, and would have cited the fact that her mother and her favorite adopted cousin were dark as proofs positive that she could not have color prejudice.

But Miss Letitia was a great believer in the white people, and the fact that they seemed to be growing farther and farther away from the Negroes made her pessimistic as to the future of the colored people as a distinct racial element in American life. She had become a convert to the theory that the only hope of the American Negro lay in finally losing himself in the white race, in being utterly absorbed. She had no sympathy, however, for such Negroes of light complexion as illegally affiliated with the white race or surreptitiously entered that race, holding that all persons with the blood of the colored race in their veins should remain within the ranks of the Negroes until the race as a whole was whitened.

On the other hand she viewed it in the light of a shocking crime for two dark persons to marry each other, holding that every newly born dark child but prolonged the agony. She felt that Providence now purposed to overrule the evil of miscegenation during the days of slavery, and to thus bring good out of evil by making use of the light complexion contributed to the race to lighten its complexion from generation to generation until it finally lost its dark hue. She was a believer in the white man's temperament, traditions, character and civilization, and did not care to see these altered by a sudden infusion of Negro blood, but felt that by the time the Negro race was ready to vanish through her gradual process of whitening, that the race would be so fundamentally metamorphosed, and the infusion so diluted that it would in no wise materially affect the base of the white man's make-up.

Miss Letitia felt that she occupied unassailable ground, as the white people could not reasonably object to her making use of the white blood which they pushed off to her side of the color line. Such was the basis of her choice of a husband for her cousin Clotille.

Baug and Clotille knew full well that they did not and would not love each other, but knowing Miss Letitia's hopes and plans, they did not jar her by raising the issue before it had to be raised, each desiring to keep the wealthy woman's favor. Operating under this *modus vivendi,* all seemed to be moving along nicely, neither Clotille nor Baug desiring to make a move, until one morning, as Clotille sat in her seat in the assembly room of Clinton College, noting the boys as they filed in to take their respective seats, she observed in those ranks a tall, handsome fellow of princely form, whose frank, open face, intellectual brow and head of splendid shape, demanded of her a second look and a third. An acquaintanceship followed in the due course of events and the exchange of sentiments in the days that followed ripened their mutual admiration into love.

One beautiful May day, a day that Clotille never forgot, in that short distance from the baseball grounds to the girls' dormitory, Conroe had poured into her ear the story of his love, and had gained from her lips, and from the depths of her tender, dark eyes the information that he was loved in return. But here is where the trouble arose—Conroe was dark.

From the day that Clotille discovered that her heart had gone out to Conroe, she began to plan to overcome Miss Letitia's objections to him. She saw clearly that her first step was to get Baug Peppers out of the way. So long as Baug was available as a possibility for a husband, Miss Letitia, Clotille knew, would be for him against the world.

The next step, as Clotille viewed the matter, was to convert the white people of Belrose to a more kindly attitude toward the colored people, for Miss Letitia was in her heart a worshipper of the whites of Belrose; felt that they were the most aristocratic people on earth. If, therefore, Belrose could be brought to the point of according the colored people the full measure of citizenship rights and privileges, it would, according to Clotille's way of thinking, operate to make Miss Letitia less pessimistic, more hopeful of the colored man's future as a colored man, and therefore less hostile to the marriage of dark couples.

"The elimination of Baug and the providing of a healthy local atmosphere for the diseased mind of Cousin Letitia is my problem, then," reasoned Clotille.

"Now, I don't know which is the harder task, the marrying off of Baug or the causing of Cousin Letitia to think that the door of hope has at last come open to the dark man," said Clotille to herself.

Time passed away, Conroe and Clotille were graduated from college, the former entering a medical school, while the latter went to Boston to perfect herself in music.

In Boston, Clotille met and studied Eina, and felt convinced that she had at last come upon the girl that could wrest from Baug the control of his heart.

Eina, who was an orphan, grew to be fond of Clotille, and expressed a desire to come to Belrose to live. This was exactly what Clotille desired, and shortly after her return home she wrote, telling Eina to come.

Now that we have seen how Eina came to Belrose, Mr. Molair may proceed to pay his visit.

CHAPTER IV.

THE VISIT IS MADE.

SLOWLY, languidly, and with ever reddening orb the sun was sinking toward its rest, making way for that eventful night in the life of Eina, when Molair was to visit her home and discuss with her the question of her racial alignment.

Hitherto Eina had looked upon the human family as one, but now was to make her choice of caste, or have the choice made for her.

"According to what Mr. Molair says, I am to half die to-night, to limit the full, free rush of my soul to the one or the other group of my fellow-beings. Whether I will or not, the choice must be made." So reflected Eina, as she sat upon her porch waiting for the set of sun which was to bring to her door Seth Molair, in charge of Uncle Jack.

When there comes the time in the life of a human being that the fate of the eternal years seems crowded into a brief space for determination, an effort on the part of the soul is put forth to burst out of its prison and ramble through the halls of nature in search of superior wisdom for a decision. So Eina looked out upon the landscape before her and said, "Mother earth, what have you to say to your daughter in this solemn hour?"

The slope that began a few hundred yards in front of her porch seemed to say "Follow me" as it gradually fell away down to a valley in which there stood a few trees scattered here and there lining a small stream that flowed leisurely along en route to the far, far distant sea.

In her imagination the meditating Eina followed the waters of this little stream, passed with them under culverts, through the city of Belrose and into the Ambrose River that skirted that city, followed the waters by the cornfields, on and on through the land of cotton, then the land of sugar-cane, by the busy wharf, by the quiet village, on and on and on to the great, great deep.

As in her imagination the waters swept out into the mighty ocean, Eina shuddered, folded her arms a little tighter as if it were she that was making the sweep into the boundless deep.

"No comfort comes to me in that line of thought," said Eina to herself, now lifting her sad eyes to the evening sky, in which the sun was all but set. But no relief was there, for the sun seemed to say, "I, too, must battle for my life."

Eina gazed at the cloud through which the sun was feebly shooting his failing rays, then looked at a heavier cloud hovering immediately beneath the fighting, dying king of day, ready to engulf him when his reign was over. At last he sank into this dark cloud into which there then came a rift through which he shot a flood of parting brilliance as if to say, "I go down, but go in the fullness of my powers. I shall rise again." The sun was set.

The spirit of Eina, yet hungry for comfort, now sought solace in the little yard before her. Rising from her chair she bent over the banister of her porch and in the gloaming looked from tree to tree and from flower to flower. The trees moved their limbs only in the feeblest manner, as if in respect for her meditation. Little birds flitted noiselessly by to their nests. Even the crickets in the grass seemed to seek to subdue their voices.

"Oh, this is too solemn. I gain strength no where. I must fight out life's great battle alone," said Eina, leaving the porch and entering her parlor.

At length Uncle Jack arrived, and with due pomp and ceremony escorted his distinguished companion into Eina's reception room.

As Molair's eye noted the carpet on the floor, the furniture, the pictures on the wall and all the little touches of art in the articles and arrangement of the room, his sense of harmony was thoroughly pleased and he said inwardly:

"No, I make no mistake when I invite this lady of refined tastes to membership in the race to which she properly belongs by every consideration of right and blood."

When the greetings of the day had been passed and a few moments occupied in conversation on general questions, Eina opened the discussion on the matter uppermost in the mind of each, and to Mr. Molair's surprise, at once put him on the defensive.

"You have come to-night to ask me to choose my social atmosphere, my spiritual home. Will you allow me to probe somewhat deeply into the matter and ask some questions that may appear impertinent?" asked Eina.

"I do not shrink from any feature of the case. I can in perfect coolness canvass the entire situation, past, present and prospective," said Molair.

"I am glad to hear you say that, Mr. Molair; so very glad. A matter so grave needs the very freest discussion. I am so glad you will not take offense. I have heard that the Southern white people were so sensitive," said Eina.

"Mr. Molair," Eina continued, "I believe the richest inheritance of a race to be its spirit. Did not slavery taint your racial spirit, and do not all who enter your portals pass under the shadow of the blight?"

"Upon the great mass of mankind, Miss Rapona, environing influences have a marked effect, but there are natures that rise superior to their environments, just as the lily in all of its beauty and cleanliness rises from the slush and slime," began Molair, in reply.

"My ancestors owned slaves, but were not in any manner demoralized by the institution. They were kind to their slaves, did not resort to corporal punishment, taught the sanctity of the marriage relation, insisted on good moral conduct on the plantation, never through sales separated a family, and from time to time emancipated such slaves as showed that they had attained unto the full stature of industrious, civilized, moral beings. In short, to *my* ancestors, whatever else it was to others, slavery was a civilizing school, and to deal honorably by those helpless people was a family principle, sacredly transmitted from one generation to another."

"Were not your people favorable to the war of secession, which, whatever its mainspring, would have resulted in buttressing the institution of slavery?" asked Eina.

"The institution of slavery was not, of course, of Southern origin. It was with us an inheritance from a world-wide custom. We happened to get a larger dose of it than any other part of the world, as our home was near the latitude of the original home of the enslaved race. My family believed the institution wrong and harmful in the large, but felt that the South could better work out the problem of getting rid of the institution alone rather than in connection with another section lacking the sympathetic consideration that flows from immediate touch with a problem," responded Molair.

"Well, you have stood your examination very well, Mr. Molair. Right gladly will I hear what you have to say," said Eina earnestly.

"Truly, Miss Rapona, there is not a spark of prejudice behind what I am to say. I confess to having strong pride of race but not to prejudice. Of course prejudice is here, but thus far it has not inoculated me."

Eina nodded her acceptance of this assurance.

"Miss Rapona, was there ever in all the world a more pitiable spectacle than that which the presence of the colored man in America constitutes to-day? His return to Africa is precluded by the fact that Africa is projected on a lower economic and spiritual plane than that to which the Negro is willing to fall back, nor would the economic forces of the South quietly submit to a general exodus even if the Negro desired. So the Negro is riveted here by the economic conditions within and without.

"In the South there is a pronounced feeling against the absorption of the race into the political and social fabric, and he is a political and social Ishmaelite, with his hand against every one and every one's hand against him by the very logic of the situation. The door of hope is closed to him. There are no stars, no moons, no suns to light up his dark skies, so far as the body politic is concerned, and his spirit must struggle with all the darkness and briers and bogs of the spiritual jungle without the cheering light of hope, which, even when unrealized, serves to make men better. To work, to eat, to sleep, to die is the utmost programme that organized society in the South offers this race."

Mr. Molair now paused for an instant as if to allow his words to sink into Eina's heart.

"But, Mr. Molair, is there no hope?" asked Eina.

"The one thing needed in the South is political co-operation between the better elements of whites and the Negroes, but the manner of the coming of emancipation, enfranchisement and elevation to high public station seems to have riveted the Negro into one party, while the terror of being ruled by an alien and backward race have chained the real strength of the white race into an opposing party. You can see at a glance the utter depths of the sentiments, passions, and interests involved and what labor it will require to emancipate both races. I see no forces at work looking to the blending of the political interests of the white and colored people, and so my voice at this stage of the storm is simply 'no land in sight.' As long as there is to be a bitter political war between the Negroes and the whites of the South, how can the condition change?"

On and on the discussion ran, Eina asking questions and Molair seeking with the utmost candor to enlighten her from his viewpoint. After the question had been fully canvassed Molair said:

"Now, Miss Rapona, you have the situation before you. Two worlds call you to-night. Which will you enter?"

Molair now stood up and bent his gaze upon the bowed head of the troubled girl before him. In an absent-minded sort of way Eina looked up into

Molair's face, while her thoughts ran out into the wide, wide world to all that this strong, vigorous young scion of the white race typified.

As Eina sat reflecting, thus ran her thoughts:

"Here stands before me power, an offshoot of that force that bade its flag keep pace with all the journeyings of the sun. Power and glory, such as the Anglo-Saxons can give, await me. Centuries of power call unto me.

"Over against this picture stands a tragic situation and present day weakness, whatever else the future may hold. In this tragic situation is my dear, dear friend. If I enter it, I shall at least have the consolation to know that I do not personally deserve whatever of suffering comes to me. Is it better for the souls of men to be under a load that is crushing, or wittingly or unwittingly a part of the crushing load?"

Eina now arose and the two stood silent for a few moments. Each felt the awful gravity of the situation.

"Just a personal word, Miss Rapona, before you decide. Permit me to testify to my respectful admiration of you, drawn from my two interviews with you. Perhaps I seem to go too far, but when nature has the conception that what is to be done must be done quickly, it works in a hurry. Note the proverbial precociousness of the child that is not to dwell on earth very long. I would much enjoy the cultivation of your acquaintance, and feel that I would be blessed with your friendship, simply. Of course, if you choose to cast your lot with the colored people, you dig between us that unfathomable Southern gulf which is not on the maps, but which is far deeper and wider than those that are," said Molair.

"On which side of this gulf is the man with the face of mystery?" was the thought that now came into Eina's mind. Was it fate that suggested it?

Lifting her perplexed and all but tearful gaze to Molair she said: "Give me time to decide."

"Very well. If you claim your place in the white race, I hope to see you again. If you choose to cast your lot with the colored people—farewell—forever," said Molair, his voice falling to a solemn whisper.

Eina shuddered. "Good-night," she said, lingering on the words. With her hand to her cheek, lost in meditation, Eina stood long on the spot where Molair left her.

CHAPTER V.

YET DEBATING.

N the night of Seth Molair's visit to Eina, his mother sat in the library awaiting his return, as was her custom when he was out at night.

"You are a little late to-night, Seth," said Mrs. Molair, as she received her son's greeting kiss.

"Yes, mother; I have just left the home of the most beautiful, the most attractive girl that ever I saw."

Mrs. Molair's heart gave a wild leap of joy. Over her life there was but the one dark shadow. Seth was her only child, was unmarried, seemed to have never thought of matrimony for himself, and as a consequence of his course had raised the fear in her mind that their branch of the historic Molair family was near its end—a thought that was far from pleasing to her. More than anything else in the wide world, this threatened extinction of the Molair name gave her deep concern. Imagine, therefore, the rapture of her mother heart when she heard the cool, impassive Molair grow enthusiastic over the charms of a young woman.

"Describe her to me, Seth," said Mrs. Molair, laying aside a book which she had been reading, and looking approvingly at the idol of her heart.

"You would really have to see her to get a proper idea of her beauty, mother. As rich as is the English language, it really has no words that fittingly portray the charms of that girl."

Mrs. Molair felt like kissing Seth rapturously, so happy was she to find him, as she thought, thus enamored of one of the gentler sex.

"Where on earth has she been, Seth, that I have never seen her?"

"Oh, she has just arrived."

"Do your best at describing her," requested Mrs. Molair with enthusiasm.

Molair now attempted a description of Eina, and the picture that he drew served to stimulate Mrs. Molair's interest in the girl.

"Oh, may it be that kind heaven has at last sent me a wife for my son," was the inward prayer of Mrs. Molair.

"But, mother," said Molair, a look of deep seriousness on his manly face; "there is danger that she will cast her lot with, and pass as one of, the colored people."

"The stars above!" exclaimed Mrs. Molair, holding up her hands in an attitude of horror and repugnance.

"Really white?" she asked.

"Her complexion is lighter than that of many whites whom we call our friends, and she can pass the finger nail test all right," replied Molair.

"Where does she come from?"

"Boston."

"That Boston! Seth we must save this girl. We must not allow a calamity like that to befall her."

"I have been to see her and sought to dissuade her. I have not thus far succeeded, however," said Molair.

"I'll see her," said Mrs. Molair, "and when I have finished talking to her she will be in her right mind."

It was agreed upon by Seth and his mother that she was to go to see Eina early the following morning.

Mrs. Molair now retired to bed, but did not fall asleep, her mind having been thrown into such a feverish state by the news which Seth had brought. The disappearance of many of the great names of the Southland was traceable to alliances with attractive colored girls, which alliances were of course denied the sanction of law, thus throwing the progeny of great families beyond the pale of law. Thus far the Molair family had made its escape, and while Mrs. Molair had the utmost confidence in Seth's character, she could not be indifferent to the fate that had overtaken other family names, that of the Gilbreath's for example.

"If this girl can pass the test and can enter freely into the white race she might become my boy's wife, for evidently she has deeply impressed him. If she abide in the colored race and a genuine attachment ripens between her and my only boy child!—" Such were the thoughts that coursed through Mrs. Molair's mind, rendering her night a sleepless one.

On the following morning Mrs. Molair was up with the sun, and was soon speeding rapidly to Eina's home. She rang the door bell and Uncle Jack responded.

When he saw that it was Mrs. Molair, Uncle Jack called into service one of his most Chesterfieldian bows, then escorted her with much respectful dignity into Eina's parlor, where she took a seat to await Eina's coming. As she noted the beauty and taste of the appointments of Eina's home, her heart warmed to the girl.

"Only a sweet, pure soul could produce an effect like this," said Mrs. Molair to herself.

When Eina appeared at the parlor door and Mrs. Molair caught sight of her beautiful face, flashing out in no uncertain way the nobility and loftiness of her soul, Mrs. Molair heaved a sigh of relief.

"If all else fails, thank heaven, here is no Morganitic pitfall for Seth, unless mother nature who chiseled that girl's brow is a miserable liar," thought Mrs. Molair, as in her joy over the type she judged Eina to be she rushed to and kissed her.

Eina could not, of course, understand the warmth of the greeting, but felt honored, for, no less than in her own case the worth of Mrs. Molair was written in her countenance and bearing.

When seated Mrs. Molair began: "Miss Rapona, I am Mrs. Molair, the mother of Seth. I have come to take up the question of your social alignment."

"I am much pleased to meet you. Your son is a noble man at heart and in life, I feel. I am so glad that I met him. Since I see his mother, I understand the source of his qualities," said Eina.

"Seth's father, child, was the finest man that ever lived," said Mrs. Molair, her love for her deceased husband not allowing even Seth to be classed above him.

But her mother love now asserted itself, and she said: "And so is Seth."

"So we have two men, each being the finest that ever lived," said Eina laughingly, in thorough sympathy with Mrs. Molair's praise of her husband and son. In the background of her mind, however, there was a third candidate for this honor of being the finest; but his case has not yet been heard—the man with the face of mystery.

"Child, my son tells me that it is possible that you may ally yourself with the colored people. Have you ever associated with them before?" asked Mrs. Molair.

"My association has all along been with the whites, save in the case of one girl friend at whose instance I am here in the South," said Eina.

"There is a faint suggestion of the dark in your complexion, no more, however, than what numerous of our best white people have. How does that come?" asked Mrs. Molair.

"I am of Spanish, Indian and Caucasian descent."

"Have you any Negro blood?"

"The Spaniards got their tinge of the dark through the Moors, they say, and the Moors are Africans," replied Eina.

"My child, you can pass for white. We do not bar those races socially that have given marked evidence of governmental efficiency. We don't draw the line on Spaniards or a brave, fighting people like the Indians. We don't object to that blood. Did not Seth tell you about the handicaps affecting the colored race?" asked Mrs. Molair.

"He did."

"Now let me tell you some things that Seth could not tell you. By the way, where is your mother?" asked Mrs. Molair.

"Passed away. Died when I was an infant."

"Father?"

"Gone, too. Lived to see me fifteen years of age, then left me."

"Poor, dear child. Do you think I am going to allow you to choose life in the Southern underworld without doing my best to prevent it?" said Mrs. Molair, now more determined than ever to keep Eina within the white race.

"Let me talk to you as a mother to her daughter, Eina," said Mrs. Molair.

"You must. I crave of you that honor."

"Your character, Eina, is formed. Your absolute devotion to all that is noble in life is written in that sweet face of yours, in those glorious eyes. Our supreme mother, nature, has seen fit to link you with the motherhood side of the human family, and you must view matters from that point. You may be blessed with a home and daughters some day, and life for a colored girl in the South is far from ideal."

"Tell me just how and tell me frankly," said Eina earnestly, leaning forward and resting her cheek upon her hand.

"A girl, the future wife and mother, has vital need of the atmosphere of protection, respect, and chivalric deference; for upon her is the human race dependent for the direct infusion into the bone and marrow of the race all that is glorious. Civilization shows that this is only done where man accords protection to woman and allows only that which is glorious to be written upon the woman soul."

"Are not colored men brave? Can they not surround the women of their race with the desired atmosphere?" asked Eina.

Mrs. Molair, who had been sitting some little distance from Eina now drew near and said, "Child, I am going to picture to you the most tragic situation in all this earth. The white man of the South has taken the government into his hands exclusively. A government is as influential in what it will not do as in what it will do. It has been clearly demonstrated that our white government will not punish a white mob. We declaim against it, try to prevent it, but we have not yet developed the capacity to punish the mob after it has succeeded in doing its work.

"The menace of the unpunishable mob stands before every colored man who seeks to hold a white man accountable for misconduct toward the female members of his family. In court, with the best sentiment of the white people appealed to, I have no doubt but that the desire on the part of the colored man to protect his home would not be crushed out; but the mob stands between him and the court. Thus the spirit of protection, which in the white man is buttressed by the courts, is in the Negro confronted with the scowl of murder on the face of the mob.

"Are not the colored men willing to pay even this price to accord their women protection?" asked Eina.

"The colored women protect the men. Knowing the menace that confronts their men, colored women swallow insults. I dislike to dwell upon unpleasant incidents in our life here in the South, and high heaven knows there are enough of them, but a girl standing on the border line, about to make choice of race, should know all."

"Oh do speak fully, do, Mrs. Molair!" said Eina.

"Well, one of the saddest cases that ever came to my ears was that of a colored lad in a neighboring county. A white man uttered forbidden words to this boy's sister. The girl fled to her home and told her brother of what had been said to her. Borrowing from our Southern code on such matters, this boy went to the home of the white man, drew a pistol, spoke his mind very freely, but did not kill.

"The next morning the white man armed himself, went to this boy's place of work, called him out and shot him down. That is what happened where a colored girl told and her brother took the matter in hand. If that girl has another brother that is concerned in her protection, do you think she will be so ready to sentence him to death by reporting insults?"

Drawing near to Eina, Mrs. Molair threw an arm around her neck and talked to her long and earnestly, laying bare experiences that had been reported to her by the colored women of Belrose. At length she said: "Now, my daughter, I exhort you to come into a race where men are encouraged to play the part of men. Will you not come?"

Again there came into Eina's mind the face of the man of mystery.

"Mrs. Molair, I shall give earnest thought to all that you have said. When the debate within my soul is over, I will render my decision."

Mrs. Molair now arose and took a hurried leave. To her mind there was no possible ground of debate as to whether it was best to be identified with the life of the white people of the South socially, and the fact that Eina, with conditions made plain tc her, could stop to debate the question, convinced her that Eina must be suffering from some form of mental derangement.

"Why, good morning," said Mrs. Molair, backing out of the door, looking intently at Eina as at one who had lost her reason.

CHAPTER VI.

SHE INVESTIGATES.

"THIS is awful! This is simply awful!" Thus murmured Clotille Strange as she stood upon Eina's porch stung, dazed, irresolute as the result of the reading of a little note from Eina which Uncle Jack had handed her at the door, instead of granting her admission to see her friend.

The sympathetic Uncle Jack had surmised that all was not going well, and his funereal countenance as he met Clotille had been in keeping with the sombre news contained in the note, although of course he knew nothing of its contents. He now stood pitying in his heart the perturbed Clotille and resolved to be of assistance to her if he could. As Eina was in the house within hearing distance Uncle Jack could not say what he desired, so he resorted to a ruse to get an opportunity to whisper to Clotille.

"W'y Miss Clotille, look at yer harniss. Who hitched up fur yer?" said Uncle Jack loudly, moving off towards Clotille's buggy and beckoning for her to follow. Going to the far side of the horse and having Clotille do the same so that Eina, if peering through the window blinds, might not see what was going on, Uncle Jack tinkered with the harness while Clotille read to him the little note from Eina, which ran as follows:

"My Own Dear Clotille.

"You know how dearly I love you and how I crave your companionship. You will understand, therefore, that there is tremendous pressure on me from some source to prompt me to deny myself the boon of your companionship for some days—just how many I cannot say. When we meet I will explain all. For the time being I must have solitude, must travel to the very heart of things and let my darkened soul catch for itself the light of life. The world confuses me, but I know that there is peace somewhere. Whatever else betides, I am Clotille's one friend,

"EINA."

"I understan's it all now. Dem Molairs hez been wukin' on her. Mistah Molair wuz heah las' night an' Missus Molair wuz heah dis mornin'. She's fine blood an' dey wants her in dare race I 'specks. Deys 'bout got her min' sorter mixed up an' she 'bout doan' know whether ter be er white lady er er colored 'oman, es dey puts it. 'Twouldent s'prise me if dis heah same lady ain't some queen er nuther passin' roun' under some 'sumed name," said Uncle Jack, nodding his head knowingly.

"Oh, is that it, you think?" said Clotille, beginning to grasp the meaning of the note which had been handed her.

"But I'll watch dem Molairs. Trus' dat ter me. I's goin' ter slip Baug Peppers out heah an' ef he gits er chance he'll switch things back."

Clotille felt like hugging and kissing Uncle Jack. In fact, to tell the truth on the sad, yet happy, girl, she did that very thing. At the very moment when she felt her structure crumbling in a most unexpected manner, here was dear old Uncle Jack to prop it up.

Nothing could be more damaging to Clotille's hopes than for Eina to cross over into the white race, for then she would be far removed from the possibility of marrying Baug and taking him out of her way.

Assured by Uncle Jack that he would watch over Eina and seek to thwart the purposes of all who sought to have her turn her back on the colored world, Clotille rode home with a somewhat lighter heart than that which had throbbed in her body immediately after reading Eina's note.

Eina was puzzled. She soon made the discovery that Baug Peppers affiliated with the colored people socially and her great desire to unravel the mystery of his face threw itself on the side of her entering the colored race.

"But does this man do himself justice to remain classified as a Negro? He could go elsewhere and pass for white easily. Would I not be doing right to become acquainted with him and persuade him for his own good to go to some other part of the world and pass as a white man?" asked Eina of herself.

Eina now decided to go deeply into this question of race, and for the time being to withhold herself from social affiliation with either race. She came to the conclusion that through the untutored Uncle Jack, a child of nature, she would seek to get at the real essence, the ground work of the Negro soul, its basal philosophy of life. She decided, therefore, to encourage Uncle Jack to talk, to enter with zest into his chatter and to have him thus in artless fashion lay bare his soul.

In keeping with this purpose, one afternoon when Uncle Jack's work was done and he was sitting in a chair in the back yard, under the shade of a tree, with his legs crossed and a pipe in his mouth, Eina drew near, dragging a chair with her. She took a seat in front of Uncle Jack with a view to having him entertain her, while she studied him and through him his kind.

"Uncle Jack, one thing has always somewhat puzzled me. When the Civil War was going on, why did you colored people stay in the fields and feed the armies that were fighting to keep you in slavery?" asked Eina.

"Wal, Miss, I kaint speak fur de res' uv de cullud folks. I kin sorter 'splain ter yer 'bout myself. I 'membah wal whut er fix I wuz in w'en de war broke out. Suah, dar wuz er mighty wrestlin' in my heart. Yer see I allus 'preciated good treatment. Er dog 'ull do dat. Wal, my ole massa an' ole missus sartainly treated me wal, treated me wal. Miss, I didun't hab none uv de hard times I heah udder cullud folks talkin' er bout. But bless yer life, honey, some uv 'um had 'um an' had 'um bad, too. Yer see, I b'longed ter quality white folks, shuah 'nough ladies an' gemmens, an' dey's allus nice! See?" Uncle Jack arose, lowered his head respectfully to one side and said with humility, "Miss Eina, I ain't as ellerquent wid dis pipe ez I would be ef I had er chaw uv terbacky. Ef yer please, I'll go git me er chaw."

Eina excused him to prepare for a more eloquent delivery. Duly equipped Uncle Jack returned and resumed his story.

"I wuz 'splainin' 'bout whut er fix I wuz in w'en de war broke out. Ef evah I felt like cryin' w'en I didun't, it wuz w'en I wuz hòldin' massa's sturrup ez he wuz mountin' his war hoss ter ride ter de army."

"Cry for what, Uncle Jack?" asked Eina.

"Three things in one. Fust, 'cause he wuz goin'. Secon', 'cause his goin' kep' me frum goin' ter fight ergin him. Third, 'cause my missus an' her two dorters wuz so sad lak."

"How do you reconcile those sentiments, Uncle Jack, and how did his going affect your going? It would seem that his going would have made your going the easier."

"Yer doan' understan' cullud folks, miss. Our hearts tek in de good frum ev'ry sose. My massa had been kin' ter me, so I hated ter see him leave. I wanted ter be er free man an' ter he'p dem dat wuz tryin' ter free me. Wid him leavin' I couldn't go, caus' harm might er come ter my missus an' her two dorters. Ef I could 'uv got er way fust, ez I wuz tryin' ter do, de 'sponserbility uv de fambly would er been on him, but ez he beat me ter it de 'sponserbility wuz on me, an' I had ter stay."

"But, Uncle Jack, somehow I thought that you were a soldier. How do you account for your military carriage?"

"Hah, hah," laughed Uncle Jack, his dark face beaming with pride. "No, miss, yer is er leetul wrong dare. I ain't got no miluntary kerridge an' ain't had none. I seen ole Genul Grant ridin' in one wunst, but I nevah got so high ez ter hab er kerridge. I ain't nebbar had er miluntary kerridge."

Eina smiled at Uncle Jack's misapprehension of her remark but did not enlighten him as to her true meaning.

Uncle Jack sat for a few seconds musing upon the exaggerated reports of his generalship that had evidently gone North, to be picked up by Miss Eina.

"Goin' back ter whar I lef' off," Uncle Jack resumed, "ole massa rode erway. I stayed behin' an' looked atter der wimmins wid er eagle eye. Ole missus b'lieved in Jack, b'lieved in him wid all her soul. I slep' at her do' w'en eber de Yankees wuz er round. Yes, dey b'lieved in Jack. An' fore God, I'd er died lak a cur dog fo'e I'd er let any scoundrel tech er stran' uv hair on enny uv 'um's head."

Uncle Jack now paused and dropped his head. Tears came streaming down the old man's cheeks.

"What is the matter?" inquired Eina, anxiously.

In broken tones he said: "I did wanter so bad ter han' ole missus an' her chillun back ter ole massa jes' as he lef' 'um wid me, but wuk an' pray, pray an' wuk ez hard ez I could, dey jes' wouldn't stay in de worl' till ole massa got back. Dey took sick one by one an' died. Oh, ef I didn't pray an' groan for de Lawd ter spar' 'um, no botty evah did. I wanted 'um ter live ter see ole massa ergin so dey could tell him how good an' kin' Jack wuz. But dey died; dey died."

Uncle Jack's chin fell over on his breast and the tears rolled down his black face with as much fluency as though those mourned were of his own family and their corpses were even then in the next room.

CHAPTER VII.

THE PARSON FLEES.

EINA arose and went into her room to think over what Uncle Jack had said.

"It would seem to me that a people with the kind of heart indicated by this old man cannot at base be bad," mused Eina. "I doubt whether anywhere in the world its kindliness of spirit can be duplicated," she reflected.

She determined after supper to probe deeper into Uncle Jack's heart.

In due time Uncle Jack summoned Eina to her supper, which was so well prepared that it stimulated her rather feeble appetite. As Uncle Jack stood by and observed that his cooking pleased Eina, a smile of deep satisfaction came upon his sober face.

"Uncle Jack, you were once a slave, but you seem to be as serene as an angel now. How did you manage to get along? Your nature does not seem to have been at all soured."

Uncle Jack dropped into a chair in the corner of the dining-room and said:

"Dare wuz er little sumpin' dat I perscivered w'en I wuz er kid dat he'ped me outen many er tight place," began Uncle Jack. "I allus did have er way uv notussing things an' puttin' one an' one togedder. Ez er boy, I notussed dat dare warn't nevah no harm in er white man ef you could jes' git him ter laf right good' an hard. Ef yer will let me, I will gib yer er sample uv how I could allus make my git by.

"Wal, w'en I wuz er youngster I wuz de house boy an' allus had ter wait on de tabul.

"One Sunday de ole missus an' her two dorters went visitin' an' lef' only de ole man at home. Wal, we had duck fur dinner dat day. I knowed ole massa wouldn't eat but one leg, so I pitched in an' cut one leg off, jes' ez smooth an' nice, an' et it up 'fore dinner.

"Yer see, I allus carved de duck, an' ez dare wuz only one leg ter be called fur, dare would be no missin' uv de udder leg. Massa nevah et more dan one duck leg at er meal.

"Wal, all wuz goin' 'long nice untel er few minutes 'fore dinner. Here comes erlong ole Majah Dinkins an' his boy ter visit us. Wal, sah, I could 'uve choked dat kid fur comin' tell he wuz blue, fur he had et wid us erfore an' he allus called fur er duck leg, w'en we had duck. W'en I saw dat boy I begin ter trimble in my boots, fur I knowed I wuz shuah goin' ter hab trouble.

"At las' ev'ry botty wuz 'roun de tabul, an' de duck wuz bein' passed 'round. One leg had been handed out ter ole man Dinkins, an' w'en de boy wuz retched he wuz axt whut he wanted. 'A leg, please,' squealed de leetul villun in er pipin' voice. Shuah, miss, I tell yer I could 'uve choked dat chap almos' ter def.

"I had stood lookin' kinder mad at him, tryin' ter sorter skeer him, so he'd be 'fraid ter eat whut I'd cooked, but he didunt bluff 'tall. Wal, dare I wuz. Ole massa, he looked all 'round de duck an' den hollered, 'Jack, whar ez dat udder leg?'

" 'Massa, ter tell yer de truf, dat duck didun't hab but one leg,' " sez I.

" 'Wal, we'll see 'bout dat atter dinner,' said ole massa.

"W'en dinner wuz ovah, ole massa, Majah Dinkins, his boy an' me went down ter de pawn whar de ducks all wuz. On our way down dare, ole massa said ter me, 'Now yer got ter show me er nudder duck wid jes' one leg er else dare is trouble brewin.'

"Wall, sah, yer may jes' guess how I wuz feelin'. My heart wuz goin' pitty patty, pitty patty.

"As de Lawd would hab it, w'en we got ter de pawn ev'ry las' duck wuz standin' on one leg wid de udder leg hid.

"Sez I ter ole massa, kinder quiet lak, so I wouldn't skeer de ducks, 'Now, Massa, whut'd I tell yer, ev'ry duck heah is got one leg.' Ole massa hollered right loud, 'Shew! shew!' an' ev'ry duck drapt de udder leg frum under his wing. 'See thar, Jack, I got yer, I got yer,' sez ole massa.

" 'Now, hole on, massa; hole on, lemme axe yer jes' one qusshun, jes' one qusshun, massa,' sez I. Dem ducks showed de udder leg w'en yer said 'Shew! Shew!' Now, massa, did yer say 'shew! shew!' ter dat duck on de tabul?

"Ole massa lak ter laf fit ter kill hisself, an' ole Majah Dinkins jes' stood up an' hollered. De kid looked fus' at ole massa, den at his papa, an' den at me. I didun't hab nothin' agin' him den, 'cause w'en ever massa could be got ter laf, trouble wuz all ovah.

"An' w'en yer come ter think uv it, de powah uv de cullud man ter start er laf hez kep' down er worl' uv trouble in dis Souf lan'. De elluphunt pertecks hisself wid his snoot, de dog makes his gitby wid his teef, de bee makes yer 'speck hisself wid er sting, an' de cullud man hez been takin' keer uv hisself wid er joke, at leas' dats de way *I* got er long mos'ly."

When Uncle Jack had finished his narrative he dropped his head and seemed to be engaged in meditation of some humorous incident, judging from the chuckle that now and then escaped. Eina sat waiting for him to share with her that which was amusing him, but when it seemed that he was going to have all the laugh to himself, she said:

"Now, Uncle Jack, that is hardly fair. Share with me. At what are you laughing now?"

"Dare wuz er thing I done wunst w'en I wuz er boy dat I ain't nevah got ovah, Miss Eina; nevah hez," said Uncle Jack.

"Now what is that, Uncle Jack? One would think from your solemn face that you had always been good," said Eina.

"Dare is whar my face ain't 'zackly curreck den, miss. I had my sheer uv 'ole Nick' in me.

"Now fur an ercount uv my bad doin's. My ole massa didun't b'lieve much in preachers. He wuz ergin slav'ry an' would lak ter 'uve turnt all hissen loose, but he didun't see his way clear ter do so, 'dout de ballunce jined wid him. Ole massa felt dat he jes' mus' keep up ef he didun't do nuthin' else.

"He tried ter git de preachers ter preach ergin' slav'ry, but somehow he couldn't get 'um ter tech it. Dey wuz shy uv dat qusshun 'cepin' w'en dey wuz preachin' 'Survunt 'bey yer massa.'

"Wal, ennyhow, my ole massa didun't lak er preacher fur nuthin' much, an' didun't go ter church. One day er sorter 'vangelis' preacher come through our way an' in his sermont he kinder teched on slav'ry, speakin' ergin it. My missus wuz at church dat day by herself, an' she thort dat her husban' would lak dis heah preacher caus' he kinder preacht his docterin' an' would er done more ef he had got more amens an' lesser frowns. My missus brought him home ter dinner dat Sunday, an' w'en I seed her comin' wid him I got skeert ter death. Yer see I knowed 'bout jes' whut de fambly allus et, an' some times I would tek out der remainder fust an' eat it myself. W'en I saw dis man comin' I could jes' tell frum his lean, hungry look dat dare wuzun't goin' ter be no remainder, an' lo I had done et up de remainder already. Now, dare wuz er shuah 'nough jam fur er pore innersint cullud boy. I hated ter do whut I am goin' ter tell yer erbout, but I had ter.

"It wuz er warm day an' ole missus had de preacher ter set out in de yard under er big oak. I watched my pints kinder close. Missus wanted er chance ter talk wid massa by hisself so she mout tell him dat dis preacher wuz ergin slav'ry an' he could erford ter treat him er leetul bettah dan wuz common ter him. She foun' ole massa an' took him way out in de back yard ter de grin' stone ter grin' de carvin' knife.

"While massa wuz grin'in' erway, missus tole him 'bout bringin' de preacher, an' massa fairly cussed. I knowed massa an' knowed jes' 'bout how long he'd stay hot w'en missus wuz talkin' ter him, so I 'sided ter ack at wunst. I runs out ter de preacher an' says, 'Mistah, kaint yer help er pore fambly out? Come quick.' I led him ter de corner uv de house an' said, 'Peep er 'round an' see massa 'bout ter kill missus, an' w'en he hez done done dat he is goin' ter come an' kill yer. Won't yer please go an' stop massa?'

"Jes' den massa was at his hottis' an' wuz layin' off his han's kinder wile lak.

" 'Whut he wanter kill me fur?' de tremblin' preacher axt.

" 'He doan' lak preachers an' you done come home wid his wife,' I says.

"Wal, sah, dat pore man turnt all sorts er colors. He wheeled er roun' an' shot er cross dat field lak er streak uv greased lightnin' wid me right atter him hollerin' fur life an' death. Hearin' me hollerin' an' seein' de race, massa broke out ter try ter ketch us ter fin' out de trouble. De preacher looked er roun' an' saw massa runnin' an' de knife gleamin' in de air. He twisted outen dat long tail coat, recht up an' grabbed his hat an' by gimminy, ef dat eldah didun't run ain't nobody evah run since de worl' comminced. De scriptur' sez 'Run de race wid patience,' but dat eldah busted dat scriptur' wide open, fur dare shuah wuzun't no patience in de way he run.

"Yer may not b'lieve it, but w'en dat man come ter our ten rail fence he leapt it 'thout puttin' his hand 'ter it, an' had er clear foot ter spare. Talk erbout er man bein' called an' 'spired ter preach, dat man wuz called an' 'spired ter run dat day shuah ez yer is bawn ter die.

"Wal, sah, I wuz so tickled dat I fell down flat an' had ter stuff my mouf full uv nasty weeds ter keep frum lafin'. Massa come up wid me an' axt me whut in de ——— wuz de mattah wid me. De tears wuz comin' outen my eyes. Dey wuz tears uv lafin', but massa thort dey wuz tears uv sorry. I tole massa er lie. I tole him dat de preacher wuz so hungry dat he wuz feert dat he wouldn't git ernough eatin' wid de ballunce an' dat he took an' stole de fattis' chicken an' run off wid it. Den massa wuz mad shuah 'nough an' he tole missus ter nevah bring er nuther preacher ter his house.

"Ez fur de chicken, I had et de remainder ez I tole you, an' I had hid de ballunce ter make de tale on de preacher pan out all right. W'en I got er chance I got de ballunce uv dat chicken an' sent it ter keep company wid de remainder whut I had already et."

CHAPTER VIII.

UNCLE JACK'S CONVERSION.

WHEN Uncle Jack was through with his narrative he began to clear away the dishes, Eina remaining to keep him company the while. When this task was over, Uncle Jack said: "Miss Eina, ef yer doan' keer I'll sing er hime an' hab er prarr wid yer fo' we goes ter our restin' places."

Eina assented and the two now bowed while Uncle Jack prayed. In his prayer there was manifest the simple faith of a child, a belief in the miraculous power of God and his readiness to resort to the miraculous. To Uncle Jack heaven was a reality, just over the way, and as he talked of it Eina could catch the gleam of the gold on the streets, hear the angel shouts and taste of the nectar flowing from the throne of God.

Uncle Jack's plea for protection through the night and for light to souls that were 'gropin' in de dark' was freighted with all the eloquence of a plea born of a whole heart, and when he arose the tears were streaming down Eina's cheeks.

Uncle Jack very solemnly bade her good night, evidently not desiring to say or do anything that would disturb the solemn frame of mind in which he now found himself and Eina.

"De sperrit is on me an' I mus' let it stay long ez it will," was Uncle Jack's thought.

The next morning at breakfast Eina said, "Uncle Jack, tell me how you professed religion, won't you?"

"Yer axes me 'bout my gittin' 'ligion, an' I is shuah goin' ter tell yer," responded Uncle Jack.

"Yer see, Miss Eina, in slav'ry times de cullud folks had ter set up in de galluries at de white churches, an' frum dat fack an' frum bein' slaves dey kinder thort dat God had er kinder secon' han' intruss in dare gittin' 'ligion. Dey felt kind uv humble lak' an' thort it took er whole lot ter git God ter look at 'um. De freeness uv salvation wuzun't talked erbout much. De hardniss uv gittin' ter God wuz de nachel thort uv er pore slave. Dare is er heap in whut er man jes' nachally thinks, jes' nachally thinks.

"Wal, gittin' 'ligion got ter be er hard thing 'mongst de slaves, an' it wuz kep' up atter freedom. Dare wuz er mourners' bench fixed fur yer, an' yer had ter go ter dat, night atter night. Yer had ter be chased by de debbul, had ter pay er visit ter hell, had ter be shuck ovah hell holdin' ter er spider web, an' had ter pray in er grabe yard. Now, it wuz jes' on dat las' pint whar I got my fall down. I jes' couldent come through at de mourners' bench an' wuz tole ter go ter de grabe yard atter night.

"In dem days I had er fine dog name Wolf. He was called dat 'cause he looked jes' 'zackly lak er wolf. One night erbout dark I started out towards de grabe yard ter pray, an', 'thout my knowin' it, dat dog followed me. I felt all right till I comminced ter git 'mong dem trees. All dat stillness seemed ter settle right down on me, an' I could heah myself breathin', an' feel myself gittin' er leetul hot. But I sez ter myself, 'I'se goin' ter stick it out, an' run jes' w'en I kaint he'p it.'

"I started ter kneel down an' er big ole rabbit jumped up right berhin' me, an, 'fore de Lawd it lak ter skeert der life outen me. W'en I foun' out whut it wuz I furgot whut I come out fur an' cussed lak a sailor. Yes, miss, I is sorry ter say it, but I cussed.

"Wal, dat grieved me ter my heart. Den I 'termined dat I wuz shuah boun' fur hell ef I didun't do sumpin'. So I gits down on my knees an' shets bofe my eyes right tight. But ter save my life I couldn't think 'bout God fur wonderin' whut mought be movin' 'round in de grabe yard nigh unter me. Now, heahs how I come ter allus b'lieve dat a man should be one thing or tuther. I tried ter d'vide up twix' God an' myself. While bofe eyes wuz still shet I 'grees wid myself right quick ter compermise wid my skeert feelin's an' keep one eye shet fur God's sake an' one eye open fur Jack's sake. I opened one eye an' lo! dare wuz standin' right en front uv me whut looked lak er great big wolf. It wuz my dog ter be shuah, but ez I looked at dat animule I forgot dat I evah had er dog in de worl'.

"Talk erbout er man's bein' skeert, dat' ain't no name fur whut I wuz. I thort dat wolf wuz de very debbul hisself come atter me for sinnin' an' cussin'. Holler? W'y, 'oman, dem dead folks ain't goin't ter heah no more sich hollerin' ez I done till Gabrill hisself makes de noise. An' ter tell de trufe he'll hatter blow dat trumpit mighty loud ter git by whut I done wid my nachal mouf. An' de way I hollered skeert me ergin. I sorter feert dat any sleepin' ghost jes' mus' er heered me. An' ef evah yer saw er man run, dis heah cullud man whut yer see heah shuah did run.

"Atter I had got er good ways er long I kinder looked back an' dare wuz dat debbul right berhin' me. Wal, sah, frum dat time on it wuz runnin' an' hollerin' an' hollerin' an' runnin'.

"I broke right straight fur de church whar de people wuz all getherin'. Dey heered me comin', an', 'owan, de noise de folks did make shoutin' fur joy wuz er sight! Yer see dey thort I'd dun come through. Some uv de sisterin' in dey joy tried ter meet and ketch me, but I kep' comin' tell I got plum in dat church an' fell on de floor. W'en I come ter myself dey wuz all eroun' me clappin' han's and shoutin' fur joy.

"Now, I knowed dat dey would be 'spectin' me ter do sumpin' w'en I got up. So I jes' said 'taint no harm ter say, 'Glory ter God!' So I hopped up clappin' han's, sayin', 'Glory to God!

Glory ter God! Wal, dey all tuk it dat I wuz converted.

"I let it stan' dat way ter keep frum skanderlizin' de meetin', but I went off ter talk ter er white preacher, an' from him I got de white folks quiut kind uv 'ligion. But de cullud folks thort I got it dat night. Ef bein' skeert uv whut I thort wuz de debbul is gittin' 'ligion, den I more'n got it dat night, I tell yer. But ef turnin' yerself loose bodaciously an' sperritually ovah ter de great God uv heben an' losin' whut yer want ter do in whut he wants done, den I mus' say dat my 'ligion 'rived ter me later on w'en I made er pint blank s'render in my heart."

CHAPTER IX.

THE MAN APPEARS.

UNCLE Jack was by no means a fool, and soon divined that Eina had some deep purpose in having him talk. His thorough knowledge of conditions in the South, the visits of Seth Molair and his mother, Eina's letter to Clotille, together with that sad, anxious look which Eina was wearing on her face fully assured Uncle Jack as to the great battle that was being fought out in Eina's mind.

True to his promise to Clotille, Uncle Jack planned to introduce the man with the face of mystery, Baug Peppers, as a factor in the contest.

"Miss Eina, I got er leetul favor I wants ter ax uv yer, please, miss," said Uncle Jack to Eina.

"Say on, Uncle Jack. It will have to be a very large favor for me to thing of refusing you."

"Thankee, miss, thankee. In Belrose dare is er fine frien' uv mine whut I wants ter come out an' see whar I am wukin'. I wants him ter take supper wid me dis evenin', an' I wants ter know ef yer will let me eat him in de dinin' room atter yer is done wid yer supper?"

"Are you a cannibal, Uncle Jack?" asked Eina, laughingly.

"Whut is er kannerbull, miss, please, miss?

"A man who eats men. You say you want to eat your friend in the dining-room."

"Hah, hah, hah," laughed Uncle Jack heartily. "Dat is shuah er good one on me. Wal, my frien' is good 'nough ter eat."

"Uncle Jack, I shall grant your request on one condition, and that is that you allow me to be the waitress for the occasion."

"Why, laws a mussy, miss! Why, no, miss. Me ter hab yer ter wait on me! Nevah, while my name is Jackson Simpkins Hezekiah Morris, will I 'gree ter dat plan."

"All right, then, Uncle Jack," said Eina, seeming to yield.

That evening when Uncle Jack and Baug had sat down to eat supper, Eina appeared at the door having on the cap and apron of a waitress.

Uncle Jack held up his hands in horror, but Baug, who had caught sight of the beautiful Eina, said, "Uncle Jack, please be civilized."

Eina looked so very pretty in her waitress' attire that Baug seemed to feel dimly that she was some sort of an angel whom Uncle Jack might drive away. Baug's admonition and a look of rebuke in Eina's eye quieted Uncle Jack.

Baug was not as a rule a hearty eater, but on this occasion he caused the food to disappear from the plates time and time again in order that he might have the waitress reappear the oftener. After Baug had eaten about all that he could possibly eat, desiring to get one more look at the waitress, he slipped the biscuits out of the plate into his pocket and called for more.

"My, Uncle Jack, this is good cooking. Is there any way, Uncle Jack, I can get out to see you a little oftener? I always thought a great deal of you, Uncle Jack, as you know. Now that you are getting old you need companionship," said Baug very solicitously, at the close of the meal.

Uncle Jack chuckled inwardly. He knew that it was the comely waitress and not the aged Uncle Jack that Baug felt needed companionship. But he appeared not to know at what Baug was aiming.

"Dis place is kinder fur out an' I mout move in closer whar you could see me of'ner, Baug," said Uncle Jack, innocently enough.

"Now, Uncle Jack, I wouldn't think of leaving a nice place like this. No, no. Stay here, Uncle Jack," said Baug, realizing that if Uncle Jack left that place there might not be an excuse for his calling at the house where this waitress was.

"All right, Baug, I'll stay. I won't go. I lak ter take yer advice." Then Uncle Jack added as if incidentally, "De girl dat waited on us won't be our waitress ennymore," consoling himself with the thought that he was at least technically telling the truth, as Eina was not of course the family waitress.

This information seemed to throw a chill over Baug's bouyant spirits, and he grew silent for a few moments, Uncle Jack watching him slyly out of the corners of his eyes.

"By the way, Uncle Jack, I may be rather busy for a while, and may not be able to come to see you as often as I thought I would a few moments ago," said Baug, falling into the trap that the shrewd Uncle Jack had laid for him.

A little later on Uncle Jack said, "Baug, I've got er good chance ter wuk at de place whar de waitress will be termorrow, but as yer 'vises me ter stay heah, I'll stay," said Uncle Jack, resignedly.

"Well, now, Uncle Jack, I am not infallible. It might be best for you to change, I can't just say. In fact, it might not hurt you, Uncle Jack, to always work at the place where the waitress works, for evidently she is a good judge of desirable places," said Baug. It was as much as Uncle Jack could do to avoid laughing outright.

"Wal, I'll tell yer whut I'll do. I'll persuade de waitress ter stay on heah er while 'tell we can see further. I knows I kin do dat."

"Now, that is sensible, Uncle Jack. That is sensible. By the way, have you a calendar?"

"Dares one on de wall."

"Let me see. Let me see. Well, no, no, no; I am not going to be so busy after all for awhile. In fact, I need a little rest. I guess I'll be out to see you often, Uncle Jack, often. I'll even come sometimes in the afternoon, Uncle Jack."

"All right, Baug, come w'en yer kin."

Baug now took his departure, and Uncle Jack went out to his stable to indulge in a hearty laugh.

"Dat Baug done et ernough fur two men ter night, an' de scamp is carryin' 'way ernough biscuits in his pockits ter start er small size bakery. I nevah seed er man so smote in my life. Fust he wanted ter come ter see me, den couldent come, den could. Fust I mustn't leave, den mout, den mouten't, all 'cordin' to whar de waitress was goin' ter be. Hah, hah, hah. I jes' twisted him 'roun' my finger.

"Now, Baug wuzun't tellin' er story nairy time. W'en er feller is in love er is fallin' in love, de worl' jes' nachally changes en er twinklin' uv er eye, 'cordin' to de 'oman. Some sez de worl' 'volves 'roun' de sun. Uncle Jack sez it 'volves 'roun' er nice, putty 'oman. Which is de bes' 'stronimy, Uncle Jack's 'stronimy on dat pint, er de jorgiphys 'stronimy?"

CHAPTER X.

CONROE DRISCOLL.

SUMMER has gone and the green of the trees has given way to the somber brown of the autumn. The students of the various institutions of learning located in Belrose for the education of colored youths (there are several such) have arrived and settled down to work.

In fact, Thanksgiving Day is here, and there is a great stir in Negro social circles anent the great annual football contest between the two leading institutions of learning. Society among the whites is also all agog over a game to be played between the leading university team of the South and the team of one of the North's great schools. So the city is alive with tooting horns and college yells and flying ribbons, and gay equippages, carriages and buggies, tandems and tallyhos, bearing happy girls and pleasant-looking matrons all wearing their best. Baug Peppers is on hand with an open barouche escorting Eina, looking her very loveliest.

At one point in the city a congestion of vehicles occurred, and Baug's carriage had to halt. It stopped just behind one occupied by Seth Molair and a lady who was the acknowledged beauty of the city among the whites.

Seth Molair, happening to look around, saw Eina, whereupon he politely lifted his hat and bowed. Eina returned the bow with a smile.

The dense crowd of white and colored people at this point, having its eyes focussed upon the two carriages because of the beauty of the occupants, saw the incident, and it created a mild sensation, it not being customary for white men to practice the amenities toward colored women.

All eyes now turned towards Eina, known to the crowd as a colored girl, because Baug was her escort. There she sat, the very essence of the beautiful, her black eyes sparkling and her rich complexion tinged with a peach's red. So innocent, so open, so noble was her appearance that every suggestion of the sinister that arose because a white man had spoken to her died on the threshold of the mind tentatively entertaining it.

As Baug Peppers drove through Belrose that day his eye wandered from face to face, and, of course, frequently back to Eina, and though Belrose had turned out its loveliest creatures, he found none to compare with her.

When they entered the football grounds they found a great throng there, and when the carriage halted Eina stood up to gaze about her. Grace characterized the demeanor of the women, their attire being all that the most fastidious taste could exact, while the men, too, presented a splendid appearance. There was everywhere an air of culture.

"Oh, who can doubt the future of this people, who can be ashamed to be numbered with them when they gaze upon a scene like this?" murmured Eina.

Baug now stood up by Eina's side, and the two presented so fine an appearance that when a squad of marchers passed that way one of the group shouted, "Three cheers for Peppers and the queen that is with him," and the cheers were given with a hearty good will.

Eina noted the abundant good humor and the enthusiasm that characterized the throng, and turning to Baug, she said: "A people so constituted that they have a well of happiness within themselves, to which they can repair when the outer world goes dry, will live long on the earth."

"Well spoken," Baug replied.

Amid the cheers of their respective partisans the two football teams trotted out on the field and lined up for the struggle. Each of the teams was composed very largely of men who were spending their last year in school, and it was realized that the struggle was to be one of the most desperate ever played in the history of the two schools.

Moving about among the players was the stalwart form of Conroe Driscoll. Of late Conroe had been urging Clotille to set a time, approximately, for their wedding, but as Baug was not yet out of the way, and as Miss Letitia was still pessimistic as to what the colored man would amount to as a colored man, Clotille, anxious, if possible, to retain her cousin's favor and obtain the fortune, was not disposed as yet to yield to Conroe's pleadings.

Conroe had learned that his color formed the basis of Miss Letitia's objections to him, and the situation grieved him sorely.

"It is a downright shame for a dark man to have to battle for the hand of a dark girl. It is an abomination," was Conroe's comment on the situation.

He felt assured that Clotille loved him, but was deeply stung that she should hold back for a moment on account of the fortune. Having brooded over his case a great deal, the day of the football game found him in a rather desperate mood. In fact, he was largely disheartened and was rather indifferent in spirit as to whether he did or did not continue the battle of life, afflicted as he was at such a vital point by a reflection of color prejudice or color handicap within his own race.

Of course there were thousands and thousands of colored people of light complexion who did not draw the color line, but what advantage was this fact to Conroe when the one mulatto who had charge of the girl of his choice did draw the line?

Conroe bestowed upon the school which he was attending a wealth of devotion, being profoundly grateful to it for having provided the way by means of which he could catch an inspiring glimpse of the upper realms of life, even if he was not to be spared to enter those realms.

It was his resolve, therefore, to yield every atom of his strength to the task of winning the victory for his team that day, and it mattered little to him as to the price that should be exacted of him, even unto his death.

The ball was put into play, and it was soon seen that the two teams were about evenly matched. The first half of the game was played with honors about evenly divided, neither side scoring. But when the second half opened it was soon apparent that some mighty force was at work on Conroe's team, and it was Conroe himself. In a manner that showed an utter disregard for his own safety, and that sent chill after chill of fear tc Clotille's heart, he played his part in the game with almost superhuman strength.

The opposing team was quick to note where their danger lay and began to center their attacks on Conroe in an effort to weaken him. The fact that he invited the attacks of the entire opposing team did not daunt, but seemed rather to please him. When called upon to carry the ball it was a thrilling sight to all save Clotille to see the manner in which he ploughed along, with the opposition in its entirety clinging to him. When the ball was in the enemy's hands, like a steam engine he broke through all opposition and tackled the one carrying the ball, only to be heavily piled upon himself by the opposition team.

How Conroe craved a blow that would kill!

"Others have died on the football ground, and why may not I?" was the cry of his heart.

Conroe's team was nearing the goal line of the opposition and the ball was given to him for a plunge. A dash, a crush, a falling down, the ball carried forward to the danger line, and Conroe lay gasping upon the ground. Water carriers rushed to him with their sponges and the doctors were summoned.

"Two ribs broken, it seems," one doctor murmured to another.

"Oh, is he dead? Is he dead?" cried Clotille, dropping to her knees, clasping her hands, her heart the home of agony.

When Conroe regained consciousness he sprang to his feet and said: "I am all right."

The doctor looked at him, saw that he gave no sign of being pained, and thought that he had possibly been mistaken. The doctor suggested that he leave the game, but Conroe said:

"Oh, go away lady doctor. I am all right. Get to your places, boys."

The two teams now faced each other for the final play. The time for the game was all but out and neither team had thus far scored. The team whose goal line was now threatened saw no opportunity to score against Conroe's team, but with grim determination they awaited this final assault, resolved to use every atom of force in their beings to prevent the score.

The captain had his doubts about Conroe's ability to handle the ball at this crisis owing to the manner in which he had been battered. He turned to catch the gleam of Conroe's eye to see whether the latter felt equal to the task.

"See that I get that ball," was the message that Conroe flashed to the captain.

The opposition team caught the exchange of significant glances and prepared for Conroe. The whistle blew, the signals were called, and Conroe received the ball.

"In this happy hour, across the goal line of the enemy, oh, heaven, give me death, give me death!"

With this prayer upon his lips, Conroe made the plunge. Like wild beasts of the forests the opposition swarmed about him, trying to pull him down. His whole body seemed to him one great pain and he felt as though a world was upon him, but somehow he did not shrink. His will appeared to have converted his muscles into iron. Supported by his team, he slowly, steadily pushed the struggling mass of humanity opposing him, back and back and back, inch by inch.

The mighty throng held its breath.

Slowly, doggedly, with grim determination, Conroe, backed by his resolute team, continued to push his way until, across the goal line, he fell to the ground, clutching the ball as with hooks of steel.

A mighty shout broke out upon the air and men wild with enthusiasm rushed to the scene intending to carry Conroe on their shoulders around the grounds.

But when the struggling players had disentangled themselves it was found that Conroe did not rise.

CHAPTER XI.

EINA BEGINS TO PLAN.

EINA had noted the desperate character of Conroe's playing, and her woman's intuition told her at once that his bearing was that of a soul struggling with some dark shadow.

Learning where Conroe was taken for treatment, Eina called on him, and by her warm, unfeigned sympathy, completely won his confidence. To her he told the story of his baffled love, how that Clotille, the girl of his choice, was being withheld from him on account of his color.

As Conroe was a noble, handsome fellow Eina divined at once that the trouble was not to be found in him but somewhere in things external to him. As she gazed upon his fine, manly face, listened to the sentiments of his heart and thought of his love for one of his own mould, from whom he was being debarred by sinister influences in American life, she then and there resolved to dedicate her life to the sweeping away of whatever barriers stood in the way of the happiness of her beloved Clotille and the admirable Conroe.

Here then was to be a battle royal within the colored race, Eina of the light complexion battling against Miss Letitia of the light complexion, the two taking opposite views with regard to the destinies of two dark persons.

Eina had learned to esteem very highly Uncle Jack's philosophizings, and now that she was about to plan for the purging of the atmosphere that there might be a larger measure of hope for a man of the dark hue and less of sentiment against him, she thought that it would be well for her to go back into the past, that its mistakes might be a guiding influence in any new movement projected.

"Uncle Jack," said Eina, one day, as she stood observing him as he washed the buggy, "do tell me how it is that you colored people and the white people have gotten so far apart here in the South. From what I can learn there was less of personal freindship after the war than during and before it. How was that?"

"Ef yer'll wait 'tell I'm done dis buggy, an' let me hab er extry big chaw uv terbacky, an'll lets take seats out heah in de shade uv de big tree, I'll make it plain er 'nough fur er babe," said Uncle Jack.

After the buggy was washed, Eina arranged the chairs and suffered Uncle Jack to equip himself with his thought stimulator. Thus situated, Uncle Jack launched into his subject.

"Befo' de war I uster heah de white men 'scussin' frein' de slaves, an' de one thing dat dey said kep' 'um back wuz dey thort dat de cullud people coulden't be kep' at wuk 'cep'in ez slaves. Dat's one reasun dat love nor money could make mos' uv de 'ristocrat white folks 'gree ter turn de slaves loose.

"Whut is rich sile wid no plow ter turn it up? Home uv weeds," said Uncle Jack, pausing to empty his mouth of accumulated tobacco juice.

"Wal, w'en 'manserpation come we uns had sevvul notions. Fust we thort ter 'joy our liburtee by restin' er while, jes' ter see how it feel not ter be at wuk some time. We wuz by our liburtee lak er leetul boy wid er new top. We wanted ter play wid it ter see how it would do. Den ergin, we uns felt dat we could 'joy our liburtee better on some udder plantation dan on ourn. Yer see it wuz mighty hard fur er feller ter stan' whar he uster be beat an' bellow lak er steer an' feel he wuz er man. Dat ole creepy feelin' would somehow come back, an' so lots uv de cullud people lef' fur udder plantations jes' ter git plum erway frum ole times. Den ergin er new man mout not feel so spry 'round yer as yer own massa.

"Wal, de white folks thort we wuz quittin' fur good, an' didun't understan' why we wuz runnin' frum farm ter farm. De cullud folks wuz huntin' fur de place whar dey could 'joy dare liburtee an' manhood feelin's mos'.

"Now dare wuz er nudder fac'. Dare wuz mo' in slav'ry' cepin' wuk. Dare wuz 'buse in it an' no talkin' back. Dat wuz er big part uv it.

"De white people 'spected ter keep up dat, but de cullud man wanted ter talk back. So w'en de legislachurs met dey brung er 'bout laws dat jam by put us in slav'ry ergin. Fac' it wuz so close on ter it dat dare wuzunt no fun in it.

"Wal atter so long er time, de Norf, seein' whut we wuz headin' towards, stepped in an' says we ain't goin' ter hab no more slav'ry ter be fightin' ovah. Dat wuz how we got de ballut, ter put men in de legislachur dat would keep us free an' 'peal back dem jam by slav'ry laws.

"Wal, de legislachurs kep' us free all right an' we at las' felt lak men dem days. But de white people sez dat dem legislachurs treated dem almos' ez bad ez I heahs de people uv New Yawk an' Phillerdelphia an' Fran Sancisco hez been treated by some white folks.

"Wal, de bes' white people didun't think we wuz fittin' ter vote an' woulden't hab nothin' ter do wid us. Wal, we jes' had ter take de skallerwags. Now, ef dare is enny one thing er cullud man do know it is de diffunce 'tween a quality white man an' trash. But ef yer jes' kain't git logs ter burn, yer jes' mus' use chips. Comin' ter de pint uv de white an' cullud people's fallin' out it wuz mos' 'bout de *plans* de white folks took ter deal wid 'um.

Just here a smile appeared on Uncle Jack's face, that smile that was always the forerunner of some humorous experience.

"What is it now, Uncle Jack?" asked Eina, coaxingly.

"I 'spec' I kin make my meanin' er leetul plainer ter yer by jes' citin' sumpin' dat happunned ter me once 'pon er time."

"All right, Uncle Jack; out with it," said Eina.

"I 'membah w'en I wuz er young buck an' fust tuk it in my head ter try ter go wid de gals. De gal dat I coated fust, dat is, dat I thort I wuz coatin', wuz er big, fat, lakley-lookin' gal, an' wuz ez good ter look at ez er nice fat pig at hog-killin' time. An' I mus' 'fess dat I shuah did lak her. She could talk lak er poll paritt, walk ez proud ez er peacock, sing lak er markin' bird an' dance lak er buzz saw. W'en evah I would see her doin' enny uv dem things it would make me feel good all ovah, an' I would jes' say ter myself, 'Ef I could jes' git dat gal, I'd feel prouder dan ef I could eat wheat bread an' chicken fur er whole month.'

"De trouble 'twixt me an' dat gal come erbout in dis way. Ez I jes' said, she wuz er talker. Wal, I wuzunt in dem days. W'en I wuzunt whar she wuz I could jes' talk ter her lak er churn dasher talkin' ter two gallons uv clabber, an' goin' splish er splash. But jes' ez shuah ez I got whar de gal wuz, er lump uv some kin' allus riz right up in my throat an' ter save my life I couldent talk ter her.

"I thort I wuz cunjured an' went ter er cunjure doctah. He told me dat dare wuz er worm in my throat dat some buck had done had ter git in dare ter eat up my wurruds, so ez I coulden't beat his time wid de gal. I done whut he tole me ter do, but de wurruds wuz et up jes' ez fas' ez evah. But I wuz jes' ez steady goin' ter see her ez evah.

De buck dat wuz tryin' ter beat my time, he would come ter see her, an' me an' him would set an' set, one tryin' ter out set de udder. Dis buck had er whole lot uv gab an' I seed he wuz goin' ter beat my time, so I jes' up an' tole him dat I would lick de stuffenin' outen him ef he showed up at dat gal's house ergin.

"De gal by dis time had erbout got plum tired uv me, 'cause I wuz kinder lak dey say Moses wuz, slow uv speech, an' she 'sided ter help de udder feller.

"De nex' visitin' time, she wuz out en er leetul grove not fur frum de house whar she wuz stayin', an' dis buck wuz dare wid her. W'en I went whar she wuz she cum up ter me an' kinder fell on my neck an' said, 'Oh, Mistah Jack, doan' fit right heah ter night.' 'He said he wuz goin' ter whup me ter night, an' he's got ter do it,' said de buck dat was my orrival fur de gal.

"W'en he said dat, I made fur him, wid he gal pullin' at my coat tail. Yer mout not b'leve it, but dat gal slipped er big dead snake in my coat pockit. Evah botty 'roun' dem plantations knowed dat I wuz skeert uv snakes, dead er erlive, an' she had kilt dat snake an' kep' him jes' fur me atter she seed de fight wuz comin'. De udder feller squared hisself an' we wuz ready fur de fight w'en de gal said, 'Laws a mussy, Mistah Jack, yer been layin' down somewhar an' er big snake done crawled up in yer pockit.'

"Quick ez er flash I retched er han' ter my

pockit, ter see ef she wuz er jokin'. Wal, sah, w'en my han' teched dat slick sarpin' down in dat pockit de cole chills jes' chased one er nudder up an' down my back.

"Talk erbout dancin,' yer Uncle Jack danced in er clean place 'long erbout den. I hollered, 'Heah, feller, help me git rid uv dis snake. Come quick.' 'Whut erbout de gal?' he said ter me. 'Plague tek de gal, I'm bothered 'bout snakes jes' now.' said I, dancin' 'roun' and 'roun', holdin' my coat tail ez fur frum me ez I could. 'Ef yer will promis' me dat yer won't bother my gal no more, I'll help yer wid de snake,' he said.

"Wal, I felt dat ef sumpin' didunt happen de snake wuz goin' ter wake up an' bite me ter death, an' den de feller would hab de gal. I thort quick an' said, 'It's bettah ter be *live* widout de gal dan be *dead* widout her; yer kin hab all de gals in de worl' ef yer will help me ter save my life frum dis snake.' Den de feller an' de gal come an' helped me ter git off my coat an' de snake wuz shook out. W'en I foun' out dat de snake wuz dead I felt so 'shamed dat I slunk erway frum dat place an' didun't go back dare no more, nevah no more.

"Now de gal had er perfic' right ter git rid er me, but dare wuz er more systermatic way uv goin' 'bout it. Ef she had jes' said, 'Mistah Jack, yer ain't got quite ernough gab fur me, an' I laks some one else better'n I doos yer,' dat woul' hab settled de whole mattah.

"Now, I says dis, an' I sticks ter it: De cullud

folks knows er quality white man w'en dey sees one, an' dey hez allus been willin' ter foller de quality folks ef dey would only let 'um. W'en we foun' dat our legislachurs wuz doin' bad, ef de good white folks had come at us right, lak dey doos ter one er nudder w'en dey fin' dat dey hez put er bad gang in, we would hab help 'um ter turn de raskils out. An' ter dis day, dey kin git us ter wuk right wid 'um ef dey will only come atter us kinder right. 'Cordin' ter my notion, den, de biggis' thing dat put an' keeps de cullud an' white folks er part is de unsystermatic way de white folks hez uv comin' at de cullud folks ter straighten out things."

CHAPTER XII.

THAT IS THE QUESTION.

THE next afternoon as Eina was sitting upon her porch reading a Belrose paper, Uncle Jack was in her front yard looking from flower bed to flower bed to see just which of the flowers demanded his attention. His kindly face was aglow with the love he felt as he moved about among these tender, beautiful children of the soil.

Eina, now keenly alive to anything bearing on racial friction, had just come across a tribute to the famous Ku Klux Klan, and the laudatory character of the reference was so at variance with all that she had heard of the organization that she read the tribute through several times and then summoned Uncle Jack to read the article to him.

As she proceeded to read, she looked up and noted such a look of woe upon Uncle Jack's face that she became alarmed.

"Why, dear Uncle Jack, what on earth is the matter?"

Uncle Jack was shivering from head to foot.

"Fur de Lawd's sake doan', doan' talk erbout dem Ku Kluxes," he groaned.

"Why, Uncle Jack?"

"Wal, I'll tell yer, Miss Eina," said Uncle Jack, now taking his chew of tobacco out of his mouth and tossing it into the cuspidor, saying, as he did so, "W'en I comes ter de Ku Kluxes I doan' need nuthin' to stimmerlate me."

"Fust uv all doan' yer b'lieve dat de white people had ter oggunize ter purteck dare wimmin folks. Nevah been done since de worl' comminced, dat is, down 'mongst our white folks. Evah since I knowed er heered 'bout white folks er white 'oman's cry hez been er army an' genuls an' cunnels an' evah thing. White folks doan' no more have ter oggunize ter purteck dare wimmins dan dey do ter have ter go ter bed at night. White men jes' nachally doos dat. I doan' know who b'longed ter de Ku Kluxes w'en it fust started an' I doan' know whut it wuz started fur, but I got jes' two things ergin 'um," said Uncle Jack.

"Now that's what I want to hear from some sober old-time colored man like you," said Eina.

"Dare ain't ben no day in dis Souf lan' w'en de bes' white folks coulden't git de cullud folks ter wuk wid dem ef dey wanted ter. De truf uv de whole mattah is dat dey jes' ain't wanted ter wuk wid us in polertics. Dat is de long an' de short uv it.

"Ef de white folks had come ter de cullud people in de right sperrit dey could hab put de wrong-doers out uv businiss. 'Stead uv jinin' han' wid de cullud people an' throwin' de wrong-doers out, de Ku Kluxes come er long ter put de cullud folks out uv polertics all together. Evah botty knows dat dare wuz wrong goin' on, but it wuz er qusshum ez ter whut wuz de bes' way ter git de change. Now dare ain't no use in nobotty sayin' de white folks doan' know how ter lead de cullud folks by peacerble means. I tells yer ergin, dey wuz jes' erbove dealin' wid dare formah slaves ez men, an' dat is whut brung de Ku Kluxes erbout."

"I think I understand your viewpoint, Uncle Jack," said Eina.

"But here wuz de wustest harm dat wuz done by de Ku Kluxes. In evah man under de sun dare is some bad. In evah race dare is some men in whom more bad gits piled up dan good. Evah race hez got some mighty bad folks. De Ku Kluxes by de secrit an' night ways dat it had, furnished er cloak fur all de bad men in de Souf.

"Dey says now dat de real Ku Kluxes wuz er quiut, lady-lak oggunerzation fur helpin' poor 'fenseless folks. Wal, de bad white folks mus' er bin kep out er de lady-lak Ku Kluxes, an' got up er diffunt kind whut run erlong in de shadow uv de udders. De lady-lak Ku Kluxes mus' er wuked mostly 'mong de white folks, fur I ain't never foun' er cullud man yit dat run up ergin 'um dat come erway thinkin' dat he had been layin' in some nice 'oman's arms. W'en de lady-lak Ku Kluxes got up dis midnight secrit way uv doin' things evah bad man in de Souf clapped his han's fur joy. Evah debbul kotched right hold uv de midnight plan, an' 'fore God it wuz de baddis' times dat evah been in de lan'.

"All de murder sperrited men, de cutthroats an' de scounuls wuz happy, fur dey could now git in dare wuk. Ah dem wuz awful times!"

Uncle Jack now bowed his head and lifted his large hands to his face.

"Did you have any personal experiences with the Ku Kluxes?" asked Eina.

Uncle Jack's answer was a groan.

"Tell me about them," said Eina.

"Wal," began Uncle Jack, "de white folks allus laked me an' I could git er fust rate farm any time. Er white farmer who wuzun't so good at de businiss wuz turnt erway frum er farm an' it wuz rented ter me. He didunt lak dat, an' ez de Ku Kluxes wuz ridin' in dem days, he got up er gang an' come ter my house. Dey shot in my house an' kilt my two-year-ole boy, an' my one-year-old leetul gal, an' shot my ole 'oman through de head."

Uncle Jack here arose and slowly tottered from the room. Out in the back yard under the tree the old man wept as a babe. When more self-possessed he returned to the room and resumed his narrative.

"Dey shot me, too, an' took me out ter beat me an' hang me," continued Uncle Jack. "Atter dey had beat me, dey wuz purseedin' ter hang me w'en er gang led by de white man I wuz rentin' frum come up an' kilt evah las' one uv um, an' got me. Dare dead botties showed dat dey wuz all de wuss men erroun'. Feelin' dat dare wuk would be took fur Ku Klux wuk, dey had come ter en' my days.

"My pore, pore ole 'oman an' leetul brats dat mout be heah ter comfirt my ole age!

"Ef de Ku Kluxes did enny good, de plans dey brung erbout, midnight an' secrit doin's, made it mighty bad fur enny cullud man who had er white enemy enny whar in de lan'.

"It wuz er pity de white folks didun't lead de cullud folks erway 'stead er 'sortin' to de midnight plan dat wuz so easy and glatly tuck up by bad people.

"Ugh, ugh, ugh! Let's not talk erbout Ku Kluxes. It's goin' ter be so much bettah when de white folks makes it up in dare min's dat dey will turn in an' try ter wuk wid de cullud folks. I sticks ter it. Good white people kin lead de cullud folks ef dey will jes' 'gree ter do so."

Uncle Jack paused awhile, as if in meditation. "Miss Eina, do yer think de bes' white people will evah 'gree ter wuk 'long wid de cullud people in de same perlittercul yoke? Dat is de qusshun," said Uncle Jack, as much to himself as to Eina.

"That is the question," said Eina, lost in deep thought.

CHAPTER XIII.

EINA AND BAUG.

EINA thought long over what Uncle Jack had let fall in his talks, and now decided that she would play the part of mediator and bring the better elements of white and colored people of Belrose together, out of which harmonious relationship there would spring more benign influences to smile upon the pathway of her friends, Conroe and Clotille.

In keeping with this purpose Eina wrote the following note:

"My Dear Mr. Peppers: Will you please call at my home at eight o'clock this evening? Sharpen your wits, for I have a serious puzzle for you to unfold.

Cordially,

"EINA RAPONA."

"Will I? Will a pig eat corn? Will a bee draw nectar from a flower? Will I call to see Miss Rapona? I should say that I will," said the happy Baug upon receiving the beautifully written note that Eina had sent him. Exactly at one minute to eight he was ringing the door bell of Eina's home. Eina was attired very simply on this occasion, and by virtue of this very fact was all the more beautiful, thought Baug.

After a brief conversation on current topics Eina plunged into the matter for which she had summoned Baug.

"I have asked you here to help me solve the race question for Belrose," said Eina, her beautiful eyes resting upon Baug with a trustful glance.

If Eina had asked Baug to blow up the universe, accompanying the request with that look of confidence, he would not have had the heart to have said that what she asked was impossible. And yet he felt that he must get the stupendous nature of the task before her.

"Some very able people say that the question is absolutely unsolvable," said Baug, taking pains by his tone of voice to have himself excluded from the group of unbelievers.

"I am of the opinion that it is decidedly easy of solution, at least so far as Belrose is concerned," said Eina.

"Let me hear you on that point, Miss Rapona," said Baug, his interest greatly heightened.

"Years of development since emancipation have produced a group of cleanly, cultured, aspiring people in the colored race. The first step in the solution is for this group to take charge of and guide the racial thought and life. It can be done, and the confidence of the people in your character and ability point to you as the one man to weld this controlling group and to link it on to the masses of the colored people," said Eina.

"The dearest compliment that was ever paid me in my life, when I reflect on the source," said Baug, feelingly.

Eina bowed her thanks and continued:

"There is a thoroughly enlightened and humane class among our white neighbors that can be reached, I think. With the colored people properly guided and working in unison with the strength of the white people of the South, you will soon have no problem."

"I really think that you have the whole matter in a nutshell, Miss Rapona. I am at your service. In fact, all of my thoughts have been turned in this direction. I can hardly say for what I have been waiting. An inspiring force, I suppose," said Baug.

"Now, Mr. Peppers, in my opinion your yoke mate among the whites should be Lawyer Molair, Seth Molair."

"Miss Rapona," said Baug, in a subdued voice, "have you noticed how very often our minds have run in the same channel?"

Pausing a moment, and looking directly into Eina's face, that he might at least at this juncture hint at the deeper emotions of his heart, he asked slowly, "What do you think is the significance of this mental affinity?"

Eina blushed slightly. "Let us discuss the psychology of our agreeing after we have won our battle," said Eina, in a tone that revealed the fact that the hour when personal questions between herself and Baug were to be taken up would not be an unwelcome one.

It was now agreed that Baug was to proceed at once to the organizing of the colored people of Belrose and the putting of all that was highest in their life in the lead. Abortive efforts extending over many years to have certain amendments to the federal constitution enforced by influences without the South had convinced many of the more thoughtful colored people that it was high time for them to inaugurate some movement within the South itself that would serve to ameliorate the situation. Baug experienced, therefore, but little trouble in harnessing the substantial forces within the Negro race in his movement. The mere prospect of an honorable way to close the long political war between the races, which had kept the South in the background of national affairs, and had operated against the Negroes locally, was hailed with delight.

The next problem, and *the* problem, as Baug viewed the matter, was to win the aid of Molair.

CHAPTER XIV.

A STRANGE LETTER.

"OW, hello! By the eternals, this thing is worth thinking about! Indeed it is! Indeed it is!"

Such were the sentiments to which Seth Molair gave voice, as, barred alone in his inner office, he laid down an anonymous letter which he had just finished reading. As was his wont when he was dealing with a matter that took deep hold upon his mind, Molair now began to walk to and fro in his office, snapping his thumb and second finger as he walked. This, his stenographer had found out, was a sure sign of an intense mood on his part and it was her rule to never allow callers to see him as long as he gave these signs of absorption. She had learned that only the gravest matters thus worked upon him and that he appreciated her thoughtfulness in seeing that he was not disturbed at such times.

"Who could have written this letter?" asked Molair. Stopping at his desk as he walked, he picked up the envelope and looked at the post mark. It was a Belrose letter and had been mailed on the day previous. The address on the envelope, and the letter itself had been written on a typewriter.

"Let me read this letter again," said Molair. He now sat down, spread the letter before him and studied it closely as he read. It ran as follows:

"Mr. Seth Molair,
"Belrose.

"Dear Sir:

"You do not know me and perhaps never will. Let me now stand to you as the voice of destiny.

"You are doing wrong. In all your life you have done nothing actively to make the life of the colored people unbearable. This is wrong and I can soon show it to you.

"What we Americans need is homogeneiety in our population. In the last analysis we ought to be a people of one type. There is no room for two or more diverse ethnic types. It works for inharmony."

At this point Molair, when he first read the letter, was very much puzzled.

The letter had opened as though it came from some bitter foe of the Negro, but this last remark seemed to point to amalgamation. With quickened interest he had gone on with the letter.

"Now, how are we to get this homogeneiety?

"We can't get the Negro out of America. The economic forces of the nation, particularly of the South, and the well known love of the Negro race for the land of his birth shut that idea out.

"We can't murder them. The eternal ages would not suffice to rid us of the accumulated strain of brutality that would be necessary for the wanton slaughter of ten millions of largely law-abiding and inoffensive people."

At this point Molair's wrath had begun to mount and his eye had sought the end of the letter, desiring to know the name of the author who, having discarded emigration and annihilation, Molair felt must be on the eve of boldly suggesting amalgamation. But the next two sentences cured this thought and intensely heightened his curiosity to know just what was to be suggested. The letter continued:

"Nor can we for a moment tolerate the thought of amalgamation, which would throw us into the ranks of the colored races and make us heir to all their disadvantages, internal and external. Homogeneiety must not come that way."

"This person must be a crank of some sort," Molair had thought at this point.

"I offer two suggestions," the letter continued, "either of which would work well, I think. First, let us pass a law forbidding all people to marry save mulattoes and white people, allowing mulattoes to marry mulattoes only, and whites to marry whites only. We have on our hands both the license system and the police power. We can refuse to license black people to marry, and can throw all of them in jail who try to marry contrary to law."

Molair here smiled and said, "The fool. Why the jails of the world would not hold the prisoners."

He read on.

"You see, our prison systems in the South are money-making affairs anyhow, and it would be to our interest to have more convicts. The men could be sent to the mines and fields and the women could be made to serve as cooks and washerwomen. Each home could have a little jail into which the cook could be put, and the food to be cooked could be handed in to her. That would solve the servant problem. As fast as the blacks died out we could fill their places with foreigners.

"The second suggestion is as follows:

"Let us multiply the burdens of the colored people until the maternal instinct within the race becomes saturated with the thought that there is no hope for the colored people as such.

"I learn that already the most profitable line of advertisement in the Negro journals is of face bleaches. The weaklings in the race are deathly anxious to lose the black complexion.

"Let us make the anxious more anxious, and widen the circle of anxious ones until it embraces the millions yet untouched.

"We can heat the race so hot with the fires of race prejudice that, without being conscious of it, it will turn against its own color. The black man will avoid marrying the black woman, and the black woman the black man. The decree of nature will go forth that through the process of natural selection the race must be whitened.

"The white man and the Negro woman of the South are free. The Negro men do not molest the white men, for the Negroes are deterred by the mob and by State authorities with machine guns. The results of these unions thrown into the Negro race can help to whiten that race. By this route we can produce a white race out of the Negro race.

"But you will say (I fancy I hear you saying it) eventually we could not tell colored from white, and that the colored could then glide into the white race imperceptibly.

"Brand them! Get a little marker and stamp on the arm of every infant, 'This is a colored person.' Have the license clerks to force all men and women desiring to wed to appear before them in person and show their arms.

"You see in this way we will get the offensive black color out of our way and yet not have any of that blood in our race.

"We could require candidates for office to canvass with their sleeves rolled up, so as to disclose a brand or the absence of it, that we might know whether they were white or colored.

"Now, Mr. Molair, give up your attitude of kindliness. Let us, I say, continue to drive the black man and the black woman, as possible mates, farther and farther apart. Create such conditions as the whole Negro race will rue the day that it was made black. Sear this thought into their souls; write it in the marrow of their bones. Do this, and through the white man, the weak Negro woman and the tendency of the race to so marry as to lighten its hue, we will eventually be rid of the hated color, black.

"For the sake of a homogeneous country don't make life easier for the colored race and thus perpetuate the blacks as blacks.

"Make it harder. Give the colored man the same rights as you do a white man, and what incentive has he to desire to be white?"

Such was the letter that had stirred such a deep interest in Molair. He hardly knew how to take the letter. Its professed tone was one of hostility to the Negro race, but he did not believe that a person with the sense to write the letter could really favor the policy of cruelty suggested. The reasoning in the letter at some points seemed profound; others were absolutely absurd. The thing that interested Molair most was the thought that the prejudice of the white race was operating in the direction at least of trying to create a stampede of the colored people away from their color.

"Well, it *is* a little unreasonable to set a man's house on fire and then tell him to stay there," said Molair to himself.

"Well, sir, this prejudice is actually operating to draw into the white race more Negro blood than would dream of getting there without its aid. I see that clearly now."

He continued his walking and reflecting.

"It is said," he mused, "that a disease which a man fears and broods over is the more likely to overtake him. Are we not, by our prejudices, the greatest breeders of discontent in colordom? In keeping with nature's well-known tendency to equip its children to cope with their environments, where color is a handicap, will its tendency not be to disappear?" The letter which had thus stirred the mind of Seth Molair had been penned by the moody Conroe who had been told of Eina's purpose to use him and who now sought in this way to open to his view the possibilities of a policy of discouragement.

CHAPTER XV.

SHE INSISTS.

WHEN Baug called at Seth Molair's office he found that the latter was at home sick with the smallpox! And as the manner in which the dreaded disease was contracted might be expected to have some bearing on his decision in the matter of such vital concern to Clotille and Conroe, it is perhaps well to state how the malady was acquired.

One morning as Molair sat in his office he received a letter from the son of a colored man whom his father had numbered among his slaves. This young fellow was in jail charged with having committed a murder, but his solemn protestations of innocence somehow impressed Molair.

The Molairs had never ceased under freedom to exercise a paternal care over all those who had belonged to the family in the days of slavery, extending this interest to their descendants. Thus though busy, Molair had felt constrained to go to the aid of the accused man. To begin with, there was a presumption in Molair's mind in the man's favor, for just as the Negroes had great faith in *their* white folks, the whites, as a rule, had great faith in *their* Negroes.

Arriving in the town where the man was incarcerated, Molair repaired to the jail for a conference. The jail was used very little for white prisoners, the most of them being able to make bond, and the jailer, having as a rule nothing but Negro prisoners to deal with, paid practically no attention to sanitary conditions in the prison.

As a result, the place reeked with filth. Smallpox had developed there, had been kept a secret by such prisoners as knew it, and it was into this atmosphere, loaded with poisonous germs, that the kindhearted Molair walked.

Molair assured himself as to the innocence of the accused man, laid the foundations for a successful case, turned the matter over to a local attorney, whom he paid well, and returned to Belrose, but not before the taint of smallpox had sunk into his system.

Deep was Molair's mortification and chagrin at having the smallpox, in view of its classification as a filth disease, and the dark thought now and then obtruded itself upon him that such was his reward for troubling himself with the woes of a colored man.

When Eina heard of Molair's illness, Uncle Jack was deputized to go and find out what he could about it. He returned, bringing the news that it was smallpox with which Molair was afflicted, and that he contracted the disease trying to serve a colored man.

Uncle Jack did not, of course, understand Eina's plans, but he judged from the look of woe upon her beautiful face that in some way it was essential to their success that Molair get well, so he decided to take a hand in the matter himself.

When his evening's work was done, Uncle Jack, with Eina's permission, drove into Belrose and halted his horse at the door of one of the nicest of the houses situated in a section of the city largely owned by the colored people. Ringing the door bell, he brought to the door an aged colored woman, a Mrs. Lucy Martin, who greeted him cordially.

"Why, it is you, Jack. I am so glad to see you."

"I is glad ter see yer, Lucy; glad ter see yer," responded Uncle Jack.

The two sat down and Uncle Jack began looking around the room at the furnishings.

"Yer got er tolerable nice house, Lucy, tolerable nice. An' yer got it fixed up putty nice, too," said Uncle Jack.

"Yes, thanks to my boy, Seth Molair, I got a good start, and have my little home and furnishings all paid for. Seth is a good, dear boy," said Mrs. Martin.

The old woman's voice trembled and Uncle Jack took another and keener look at her.

"Air yer sick, Lucy?" asked Uncle Jack.

"Oh, I haven't been feeling so well here lately. But nothing serious. Old age, I reckon," replied Mrs. Martin. Somehow her appearance did not exactly suit Uncle Jack, so he studied her for awhile, then arose to go.

"Jack," said the woman, "don't you know better than to try to leave here without telling me what you came to tell me? You can't fool me, Jack. Now out with it. You came to tell me something, you bad boy, you."

"Now, Lucy, dat's all right. Don't yer bother. Dat's all right."

"No, it isn't all right, and you have got to tell me what is wrong. I know you, Jack. It is something serious. I knew it as soon as you came to that door."

"Wal, Lucy. evah thing dat is lawful ain't allus 'spedient, yer see. So I mus' tell yer good night."

"Jack," said Mrs. Martin, "you know me. I am an old woman, and you know I have a number of white and colored children and grandchildren in this place. Some one of my children must be sick to-night for you to be here. Now, have pity on a poor old woman. Don't make me roam this town all night. Tell me so I can go straight to him or her."

"Dat is jes' why I doan' want ter tell yer. I sees dat yer constertution ain't de bes' an' yer might not be ekal ter de tas'."

Mrs. Martin did not hear the last part of this remark for she was busy getting up her nursing aprons and her favorite little remedies. At length she had all that she was looking for, and forgetting in her anxiety to tell her home people goodbye, went at once with Uncle Jack to the buggy.

When seated by Uncle Jack's side Mrs. Martin

said, "Jack, I haven't been feeling right for a week or more. I just knew that something was going on wrong. Now, Jack, since you can't outdo me, be a good boy and tell me who it is of my folks that's sick."

"Wal, ef I mus', I mus', but 'pon my honah I done all I could not ter tell. It's Seth."

"Seth! Poor, poor Seth! What ails him?" asked Mrs. Martin, eagerly.

"Smallpox."

"Father have mercy! That dirty, filthy disease in my family. Why, the thoughts of it are enough to kill poor Seth. It's a wonder he isn't dead and buried. I wish I could get hold of the dirty, lousy scamp that gave it to him. I'd wring his neck till he—he—well, I wouldn't kill him. But he'd be so near dead that he would enjoy life when he got back to it. Poor, poor Seth. And they have been keeping it from me. They knew I was ailing a little. My poor, poor boy. Mammy will be there soon. Rest easy, mammy is coming, Seth."

Thus rambled Lucy Martin, Seth Molair's black mammy, as Uncle Jack whirled her along through the streets of Belrose to Seth Molair's home.

CHAPTER XVI.

THE CRUX.

WHEN Molair had sufficiently recovered from his illness to resume his law practice, Baug called upon him for the purpose of inviting his co-operation in a movement that would give recognition to the colored citizens of Belrose as a part of the city's governing force, that would clarify the atmosphere that was giving worry to Eina because of its baleful effects on Miss Letitia, through whom it was blighting the lives of Conroe and Clotille. Inspired by the thought that Eina was profoundly interested in the outcome of this conference—this effort to win over to a cause one of the nation's brightest minds, Baug was keyed up to the point of doing the best of which he was capable.

"Before we take up your matter, what objection have you to our white primaries?" Molair asked of Baug.

"You have heard of the Irishman's comment on Fredrick Douglass, have you not?" asked Baug.

"Tell it."

"An Irishman hearing Douglass speak, was very much impressed with his oratory and proceeded to compliment him. Being told that Douglass was only half colored, he remarked: 'If half a naygur can speak like that, what could a whole naygur do?'

"Your race in England and America divides into two great, almost evenly matched parties, into active and corrective, creative and critical forces. Your Southern white primaries dominated by the one party invite in only one-half of the soul of your race. About one-half of this racial soul, already halved, mark you, may dominate your white primary, and the verdict of this half of the half soul of the race is accepted without a serious try out before the whole soul," said Baug.

"Here is a thoughtful colored man," said Molair to himself, growing deeply interested. To Baug he said, "Let me see if I catch the point of your Douglass joke. You think that for a full expression of the soul of our race we need two parties, creative and critical, that such opposite forces naturally flourish not in the same but in opposing parties just as the human family divides itself into sexes, and when we have only one party just one-half of the racial soul is at work, the Irishman's 'half naygur.' "

"Exactly, Mr. Molair. It is true that you now and then let down your bars so that a white man of a political faith other than that of your dominant party can enter and vote, but his connection with the other party forces him to come in quietly, so that you still miss *that unfettered ferment of the whole Anglo-Saxon spirit, that grand, free play of all the forces of your racial soul that has in reality been the source of the political greatness of your race.* Now just read this, Mr.

Molair," said Baug, handing him a clipping from the leading daily paper of Belrose.

Mr. Molair read as follows:

"Doubtless when the official conduct of this creature is laid bare it will reveal him as a grafter, hypocrite and dirty whelp, which would fit with his known character of a coarse, revolting, lying demagogue and disgusting barbarian, who would never associate with gentlemen except by sufferance and to their annoyance."

"Well, what about it?" asked Molair.

"That is said about one of your United States Senators, an output of your primary. Can you conceive of the *whole* soul of the white race being in travail and giving birth to such a man? That is a product of your half soul. You Southern white people constantly say that Senators like this are not truly representative of your people. They do not represent your people at their highest, but they do illustrate the fruit of your half soul system, or rather your quarter soul system of elevating men."

"Since you and our white primary system are in the ring, what other lick have you for it?" asked Molair.

"I am a patriot. I love the South. I would like to see the South take its old-time place in the councils of the nation. If we of the South continue to send our quarter soul products to compete with the whole soul products of other sections, where the white race crowns its victors after a try out before the full racial strength, we will always be behind, I fear," said Baug earnestly.

"How does this in your judgment affect the colored people?" asked Molair.

"Let me repeat what your leading paper of Belrose says about that Senator.

" 'Doubtless when the official conduct of this creature is laid bare it will reveal him as a grafter, hypocrite and dirty whelp, which would fit with his known character of a coarse, revolting, lying demagogue and disgusting barbarian, who would never associate with gentlemen except by sufferance and to their annoyance.'

"Now, if your quarter soul system produces that type of a man for a Senator, just think what your chances are for getting jailers, sheriffs, policemen, prison guards and the like, who, armed with the State's authority, have over prisoners and the public the power of life and death," said Baug.

"How do the colored people of Belrose fare at the hands of the police force?" asked Molair.

"You know, Mr. Molair, there was a time in England when a man would be hanged for a comparatively light offense, but that was long, long ago. The police of Belrose have turned the hand on the dial of civilization back, back, back to those dark days. They have actually made it an offense, punishable by death, for a colored boy or man to run from an officer, however slight the offense."

"Is that really the case?" asked Molair.

"Mr. Molair," said Baug, earnestly, "what else could you expect? With your great men gone into hiding and your weaker spirits in the saddle, elected to office without regard to the colored people, they often, oh, often, actually turn the government into an engine of oppression. Sheriffs sometimes connive at lynchings. Police often murder wantonly. Gubernatorial candidates, finding that our hands are tied, and that there are votes to be made by bitterly attacking us, do not hesitate to so do. The spirit of repression, cultivated and kept at fever heat by the seekers for votes, permeates the entire social atmosphere. Denying us a voice, the government, by the act of exclusion, brands us with the mark of a Cain, and as we go forth we find increasingly the hand of man raised against us. And I predict that, with the Negro denied a voice in the government, this fact in itself will deepen and deepen the gulf between the races. With the whites being governed by its weaker minds, as I pointed out, and with those weaker minds in charge of a race, both helpless and contemned, you may guess the rest."

Continuing Baug said: "No class of colored people in Belrose feel safe. If you knew the extent of the maltreatment of all classes of colored people by some members of the police force, it would amaze you. Brutal assaults, and murder, wanton, wanton, wanton murder of man after man has been committed and yet not even a reprimand has ever been given to those who have done the killing, though witnesses of character, white and colored, have endeavored to bring the accused to trial."

"Tell me exactly now what you desire of me," Molair said, evidently deeply moved by what Baug had said.

"Those of us who abide in the Negro race realize the disadvantages that come to us as a result of being a negligible quantity in the body politic. The type of men that comes to the front has respect for the unit of *power,* nothing else; and, so long as the Negro's face is a badge of weakness, it will be just as difficult to maintain respect for his interests with that class as it is to keep an unmuzzled horse that is loose in a pasture from eating green grass spread out in abundance around him. We desire to be a part of the government. We desire that you make the race for the mayoralty of our city and appeal to the whole body of your fellow citizens, white and colored, for support. When those who persecute us find that we have a voice in the making and the unmaking of officials we shall receive more humane treatment. Such, Mr. Molair, is our request of you," said Baug.

"Of course you know that you are asking me to cut myself off from all hope of preferment save that of a local nature. If I take hold of you here on an independent basis, I lose my party regularity. You know what that means. But that is not vital. A Molair is not dependent upon public station for a place in history. He can make his own throne," said Molair to Baug.

"I do not see the matter altogether in that light, Mr. Molair. Party and sectional lines are being less and less tightly drawn. It is only a matter of a few years before the nation will again pick its Presidents from our section, and if such men as you are put forward as candidates you will find no happier, more enthusiastic supporters than will be the colored people. Without any desire to offer flattery, I know of no Southerner better equipped than you to fill that high office."

"Thank you," said Molair, who really valued the good will of the colored people.

Continuing Baug said: "That man, white or black, who can construct a political yoke in which the Negroes and the best white people of the South may work together in harmony will deserve more than the presidency. He will deserve a place in the ranks of the immortals alongside the two other great Southerners, Thomas Jefferson, whose mind coined that slow-burning fuse, 'All men are created equal,' and Abraham Lincoln, who issued the emancipation proclamation."

"It is quite a picture you dangle before my eyes. But, preferment beyond our city life or no preferment, I have had recently a most touching example of self-sacrifice that ought to spiritually equip me for all time for unselfish service," said Molair.

Arising from his seat, Molair went to a window

and looked out while he talked to Baug, to whom his back was now turned. He dared not trust himself face to face with Baug while he was discussing the subject which had now come into his mind, for he was upon the verge of shedding tears.

When he had regained sufficient control of his feelings to permit, Molair resumed the conversation, saying: "Yes, Mammy Lucy, that dear soul who in my infancy crooned above my cradle and rocked me to sleep with her lullaby songs; who saw that my every boyish whim was gratified; who washed and anointed my bruises and comforted my childish heart when, beaten and humiliated in a fight, I fled to the shelter of her apron; who more than once, with her sympathetic nature, wooed disease from me and drew it upon herself—Mammy Lucy taught me in its fullness the lesson of human love, when, hearing of my illness, she came with her wan face and emaciated form, and took my life from the altar of death and in its stead sweetly laid thereon her own. With my heart green with the memory of her sublime self-renunciation, I am in a mood, as a sort of atonement, to forego vital interests of my own for the sake of the interests of others."

After Molair had delivered himself thus, he stood in silent meditation for awhile, then turned and walked toward Baug, and said, "Go your way. This is a grave, grave question. I must have time for reflection. I received a peculiar letter not long since that has put me to thinking on this question more deeply than ever before. I know not now what my decision will be. May heaven grant me light."

CHAPTER XVII.

MOLAIR ON THE ALERT.

IN keeping with a suggestion from Baug, Molair had decided to keep watch on the police force to find out just how the Negro population was faring, so we find him morning after morning sitting in the city court room, which was usually filled for the most part with colored people of the lower order. Besotted men and slovenly women, denizens of the slums, constituted the great majority of those on trial. Drunkenness, fights as the result of jealousy, petty thefts and vagrancy were the charges as a rule lodged against the accused. There happened to be in the group on this particular morning a nicely dressed colored boy with an open, honest countenance, and his appearance quickened in Molair an interest in him. That we may understand just how this boy, whose fate played an important part in shaping Molair's decision, happened to be on trial as a vagrant it is necessary to drop back somewhat into his history.

One day, a few weeks previous to this trial, about two o'clock in the afternoon, a crowd of people, mostly colored, had gathered around a merry-go-round located on a vacant lot in Belrose. Charlie Douglass, a colored boy, driving a flour wagon, passing near the assembled crowd, caught sight of a neatly dressed little colored girl with a package of school books under her arms. He halted his wagon, dismounted, and drew near to this girl, ostensibly for the purpose of looking at the merry-go-round, but in reality to be near the little girl that had attracted his attention.

In the assembled throng there was a drunken white man who was using profane language in the presence of a number of colored girls and women. The little girl who had attracted Charlie's attention was in the group near the man using the objectionable language.

Charlie walked up to the man quietly and said to him very politely, "Mister, please don't talk that way so the girls and women can hear you."

The drunken man turned to see who it was that accosted him. Enraged at the thought of a Negro daring to criticise his conduct, he drew a pocket knife, opened it and rushed toward Charlie.

As the lad had taken pains to speak so politely, he was taken by surprise by this sudden onslaught and had to run backward to avoid being cut. As the man kept coming toward him, Charlie, as soon as he could turn, did so and ran with all the speed at his command, the white man in hot pursuit.

The girls and women shouted: "Run, boy, run! Run, boy, run!"

The feet of the drunken man being somewhat

unsteady, he fell, and thus gave Charlie time to make his escape.

Dora Mack, the neatly dressed, nice looking brown-skinned little girl, that had attracted Charlie's attention, now made a hero of him. She thought it was so nice in him to speak to the horrid man, and the deft manner in which he ran backward and the speed that he made when he could get his back to the man, were simply fine, as Dora viewed the matter. On her way to and from school each day Dora passed the place where Charlie worked, and now took occasion to greet him with a smile whenever she saw him. He was a nice looking colored boy, even when covered almost from head to foot with flour; that is, pretty little Dora Mack thought so.

To Charlie's way of thinking, Dora was just the girl for him, and he decided to try to stand a little higher in her favor. The plan which he hit upon to advance himself in her esteem was to change his job from the handling of flour to one that would permit him to wear nice clothes all the time.

"Dora is entitled to a boy that looks nice all the time," thought Charlie.

Thus, much to his mother's chagrin, Charlie decided to give up his job. Realizing that her son, who, since the death of her husband, was her main support, was doing about as well in point of wages as a Belrose colored boy was expected to do, Mrs. Douglass, his mother, strenuously opposed the change. Charlie tried to mollify her feelings by pouring into her lap all his little savings, but even this did not heal the breach between them. Nevertheless, Charlie quit his job and "dressed up," to enjoy a few days' vacation and to be able to walk as far toward her home with Dora on her way from school as the fear of Dora's mother would allow him, Dora not being permitted as yet to receive company.

This worked all right for a few days until Charlie's employer noticed that he was simply lounging around. This employer had not been successful in getting as satisfactory a hand as Charlie had been, and he was therefore all the more vexed at him for causing his discomfort and loss by leaving. He offered the boy an increase in wages to return to work, but it was not more money that Charlie wanted just now, but a job that would permit the constant wearing of clothes nice enough for Dora's beau, pretty, tidy, little Dora's beau.

Thinking that he might be doing Charlie, Charlie's mother and himself a service, the employer told a policeman of Charlie's lounging place and suggested that it might serve as a good lesson to arrest him as a vagrant. Accordingly, one day before Dora came along, the policeman put Charlie under arrest and took him to the police station. It was thus that he made his way into court where Molair caught sight of and became interested in him.

Charlie's mother being unable to pay his fine,

the boy was sentenced to the chain gang. This was a most galling thought for him, it having been the pride of his family that none of them in any of its branches had up to that time been arrested. But that which pricked him to the very heart was the thought that Dora must know of his incarceration and perhaps see him at work with the pick about his ankle.

The carts in which the prisoners rode from the police court to the streets, from which they were to clean the mud by scraping with hoes, were brought around, filled and started off. To Charlie's dismay the carts stopped on one of the streets along which Dora always journeyed to her home. But her journey on this part of the street was only for a few blocks, and Charlie hoped that they would have cleaned off that part along which Dora came before her hour for passing, and would thus be out of sight from the point where she would have to turn the corner leaving that street.

But the day was a little sultry, and those in the chain gang were not disposed to work very rapidly. Charlie worked very hard, doing about as much work as any three of the others in his eagerness to have the gang through with Dora's part of the street ere she came along. But his course in working so rapidly displeased his easy-going fellow-prisoners, and they worked all the more slowly because of this fact.

As time wore on it began to look as though they were not to do the amount of cleaning desired by Charlie, and desperation and despair settled over his young heart. His wild, nervous look, his constant glancing around as if expecting something, the dark brooding that his face revealed, his working ahead of his companions, attracted the attention of Sherman Elliott, the white guard, who, unknown to Charlie, was keeping a special watch on him.

Glancing down the street Charlie saw a group of high school children coming. The pick which he had around his ankle was much worn, his keen eye having noted this defect when choosing the one to put on. He felt that the pick could be broken if one was but willing to stand the jar of the lick necessary. Moving to the curbing, Charlie dashed the pick against the stone and sundered it. Away Charlie bounded, thinking only of Dora and desiring to be out of her sight as she passed the chain gang. The guard who had been watching for this moment, lifted his gun and fired, wounding Charlie in the back. The boy fell forward on his face and a number of bystanders rushed to him to lift him up.

"Don't—don't turn my face up. Dora, Dora, Dora!" murmured Charlie.

Thinking that turning him over might perhaps hurt him, the men followed his request and allowed him to lie with his face downward, while they telephoned for an ambulance.

"She won't see; she won't see," murmured Charlie, faintly, his face still toward the earth.

Slowly the smile of satisfaction over the fact that Dora would not see and know him faded from Charlie's face and the little fellow passed into eternal silence. If the passing Dora looked upon his lifeless form he at least did not know it.

Sherman Elliott's shot and the fact that there was not the slightest effort to molest him decided Molair's course, and he crossed the Rubicon.

CHAPTER XVIII.

KICKED OUT.

IN the campaign that followed Seth Molair's announcement as a candidate for the mayoralty there was a development in the political situation which neither Molair nor Baug had foreseen, and which served to complicate matters far beyond their anticipation.

The "organization" of the dominant party, heretofore fearing no appeal to the larger sense of the community, being confident that the one party sentiment would hold it in power regardless of the mental and moral calibre of its candidates, had uniformly preferred to put forward men of the weaker mould who might be the more easily used as puppets. But the moment it became known that Seth Molair was to try for the mayoralty, independent of "organization" influences, the "organization" saw at once that heroic action was required.

The offices for years ahead had been parceled out, but they now deemed it advisable to withhold the candidacy of the weakling whom they had designed for the mayor's chair, and to nominate a man of the Molair type. Thus Molair found himself pitted against a far stronger personality than either he or Baug had calculated upon.

The contest was truly one of the most exciting in the history of Belrose. It seemed that the cleansing, testing, developing influence of a genuine battle, the very life-breath of other sections had at last come to this hitherto complacent, if stagnant (so far as political thought was concerned), city of Belrose.

When the campaign was at its height and it was discovered that the whites were so evenly divided that the Negro vote constituted the balance of power, it was agreed by "organization" influences that an effort should be made to draw the support of the Negroes away from the Molair ticket.

In view of the long record of hostility to the Negro voters on the part of the "organization," no hope was entertained of having large numbers of them to suddenly change and come to its rescue, so money was furnished to an element of whites that manned the party under whose name the bulk of the colored people usually voted, to the end that a ticket bearing the old name might be brought out to withhold Negro support from Molair.

One Hon. Thomas Barksdale, perennial candidate for the postmastership of Belrose, was commissioned to harness the Negro voters to this decoy movement. A group of Negro ward politicians was summoned to a conference with the Hon. Thomas Barksdale, and Uncle Jack, hearing of the conference, decided to be present. At the appointed hour the committee of Negroes put in its appearance at Barksdale's office.

Uncle Jack who prided himself upon dealing with none but "quality white folks" looked with manifest disgust at the surroundings. Barksdale's office was without carpet, the desk antiquated, the library of books disarranged, the whole wearing an unkempt appearance.

Tilted back in a chair, a great, sickly, soulless smile upon his face, sat the Hon. Thomas Barksdale, having upon his head a once high beaver hat upon which, it would seem from its appearance, some Goliath of Gath had sat, and which some little David had subsequently tried to straighten. His smile disclosed the ragged remnants of his teeth and at the same time allowed two slight streams of tobacco juice to ooze out of the corners of his mouth, anointing the ends of his sandy mustache, which, shaped like the claws of a crab, nestled near his jaws.

When ready for the conference, the Hon. Thomas Barksdale stood up, bringing in bold relief his tall, angular frame, his ill-fitting Prince Albert coat, his pantaloons, baggy at the knees but a little shirky about reaching well down to this statesman's very broad foundation.

"We are all here, I suppose," said the Hon. Thomas Barksdale, in that peculiar drawl common to the uncultivated whites.

"We is," responded Uncle Jack, who, to the surprise of all, assumed the role of spokesman.

"I've summoned you here to tell you colored

folks that now is your chance," said the Hon. Thomas.

"Oh, thank you, sah; thank you, sah," said Uncle Jack, effusively.

The Hon. Thomas drew near one of the group, laid a hand on his shoulder familiarly, closed an eye, and with the index finger of his free hand began to wax eloquent.

"Yes, sir, your day has come. There is some of us who have fit, bled and died, standing up fur your people," said he.

"Yes, sah; yes, sah," said Uncle Jack. "Jes' ez yer says, some uv yer hab fit, fled and flied for us cullud folks."

The Hon. Mr. Barksdale opened his other eye to see if he was quite correct, for he fancied he had caught a note of sarcasm in Uncle Jack's voice. But Uncle Jack's countenance seemed so sober that the Hon. Mr. Barksdale decided that he was mistaken. He therefore closed the eye again and proceeded:

"We set you all free, you colored people, and we are going to stand by you to the last."

"Yes, sah, I hez heered yer riccord in de civul war 'scussed ergin an' ergin, but I allus heered dat yer had de riccord ez er runner an' not as er stanner," said Uncle Jack, humbly enough.

The Hon. Mr. Barksdale brought his closed eye back into service, dropped his hand from the man's shoulder, and stepped back a little.

"Now, I can explain that record. You see I knew that the Yankees needed spies in the South, and that is why I put on dresses during the war, and there were things that I knew, that nobody else knew, and if I had got killed, what would have become of my knowledge? So whenever a fight came up, just for the sake of my country, I always sacrificed my keen desire to fight and ran so as to preserve my knowledge for the benefit of the country. I hated to run, but as I said, I sacrificed my feelings for my country."

"Takin' dat view uv de mattah an' jedgin' frum de speed dat yer air said ter hab made in gittin' out uv Belrose w'en de sojers come in, yer wuz sartainly one uv de greatis' dat is, at leas' one uv de swiftis' paytruts dat de war purduced," said Uncle Jack.

Uncle Jack now subsided and allowed the Hon. Thomas to submit his proposition. When he had finished, the appointed spokesman of the group, who had been well groomed by Baug, said:

"Mr. Barksdale, we have followed the lead of men of your station in life for several decades. Under your leadership we find the Constitution nullified, segregation practiced, official maltreatment in full swing. You have been powerless to influence the situation. Another class of the whites has been found to work with our leaders and we are going to see what they can save from the wreck. We would to God the whites had consented sooner to work with us and had not left us to the mercies of those who sacked the State government, escaped with the loot and left us with the odium. Goodbye."

As the Negroes filed out, the Hon. Thomas Barksdale stood with his mouth wide open in astonishment. Uncle Jack was the last to leave, and the Hon. Mr. Barksdale had so far recovered his self-possession, or had so much the farther lost it, that he administered a kick to Uncle Jack.

"Hah, hah, hah; dat's 'bout whut forty years uv servin' hez brung our people frum de pie counter man; er kick out," said Uncle Jack.

CHAPTER XIX.

TIGHT PLACE FOR UNCLE JACK.

"'LL never believe it! I'll never believe it! until I see it with these two eyes of mine, and then I'll doubt it," said Miss Letitia.

"Well, cousin, you will see. Seth Molair has pledged it, and he is a man of his word," responded Clotille.

"Yes, but Seth Molair is just one man, even if he is the mayor of Belrose. The idea of the white people of Belrose tolerating colored men on the fire department! They will never do it," said Miss Letitia.

"Cousin, you are too hard. I know two Southern cities in which white people teach colored children in the public schools. I know three Southern cities in which colored men are on the police force," replied Clotille.

"Yes, but that isn't Belrose. When the white people of Belrose put colored men on the fire department I will know that the millenium is nigh at hand," said Miss Letitia in such a manner that Clotille knew that she desired the conversation to close.

Upon his election to the office of mayor, Seth Molair had asked Baug to name him some arm of the public service in which he would like to see colored men employed.

Baug had conferred with Clotille and she had suggested the fire department. Clotille knew of Miss Letitia's ardent admiration for fire fighters, and felt that if colored men could be gotten on that department it would serve to make a deep impression upon the mind of her cousin and cause her to feel that after all that which seemed impossible could come to pass. So, when Baug brought to Clotille the assurance that a colored fire company would be established she conveyed the information to her cousin, and we have seen how the latter received it.

But even the doubting Miss Letitia could not hold out against a fact, against the testimony of her own eyes. When the necessary building had been erected and the company installed, Miss Letitia would pass by the place several times a day to catch sight of what she regarded as one of the marvels of the age. When she would awake in the morning her first act would be to attire herself and walk over to the colored fire company's engine-house, as if to see whether or not it had been carted away during the night. Though bitterly opposed to the use of bicycles on the part of women, Miss Letitia bought one and learned to ride, so that she might be able to follow up fires and see the colored firemen fight the flames.

When at last Miss Letitia did see the colored firemen actually fighting the flames, her enthusiasm knew no bounds, and Clotille felt that at last the pessimism with which her cousin was afflicted now had a chance to pass away.

But this very success (the establishment of harmonious political relations between the races resulting in the colored fire company) had raised another difficulty. Miss Letitia was so elated over the new company that the very thought of ever losing it affected her greatly. She realized that it was the Negro's wise course in the matter of voting that had secured the company, and she, therefore, became deeply concerned about the right to vote.

"Oh, I am so afraid that some of those old disfranchising laws will come here some day and upset all this nice work. I will never feel safe until the Supreme Court has spoken against the discriminating laws in other States. If that could be brought about, I believe I could sleep at night."

It was thus that Clotille discovered that she had a new and grave problem on her hands.

Straight from the interview with her cousin, in which this new-found impediment was discovered, Clotille rushed to Eina's home.

"Eina, Eina, my cousin, I do believe, is beginning to see the light. But one more step needs to be taken before our road is perfectly clear."

"Well, in the name of the blessed Virgin, let us get that out of the way. I do believe I would as soon contract to move a mountain as to get you and that Conroe married," said Eina, laughingly.

"Now tell me the next step, tell me quickly and let me get to work on it," Eina continued.

"We must wipe from the constitutions of certain Southern states such of their laws as have the effect of disfranchising colored people on account of their racial connection," said Clotille.

Eina's beautiful, cheerful face took on a sober look at this announcement, the great difficulties in the way of having the laws declared unconstitutional occurring to her.

Remembering a Boston acquaintance, eminent in the legal profession, who had given long and careful study to the legal aspects of the suffrage question, Eina forthwith communicated with him, inclosing an appropriate fee, and in due course of mail received from him a statement outlining a course of procedure which in his judgment would beyond doubt force an unequivocal declaration from the Supreme Court.

When Eina received the plan she had Clotille to call and confer with her over it, a call that the perturbed Clotille was happy indeed to be able to make. The plan outlined involved the cooperation of an illiterate Negro, and after a thorough discussion of all the probabilities and possibilities in the case it was decided that Uncle Jack was the best equipped man of their acquaintance to carry through the plan with the least possible friction and personal danger. The two girls therefore summoned him into the conference with them.

Uncle Jack thought he was being summoned to tell some of his jokes, so he came bringing his "chaw of terbacky an' cuss spit daw," and wearing a smile on his aged face. He had mustered to the fore in his mind some of his most laughable anecdotes, but the serious looks on the faces of the two young women chased away his smile and his jocular mood.

As Eina began to unfold to Uncle Jack the dire need of upsetting the laws in question, he was emphatic in his approval, nodding his head vigorously, saying "Dat's so, dat's so," and giving every evidence of feeling highly honored that the young women had called him in to help consider so grave a matter.

Eina next explained the plan by means of which she hoped to have the case so brought as to force a decision. Though not a Supreme Court lawyer, the gallant Uncle Jack assured Eina that it was the best plan ever devised.

"Now for the man," said Clotille.

"De lawyah? Uv co'se I says Baug," quickly responded Uncle Jack.

"No, not the lawyer. We can get him all right. We mean the colored man that will carry out this plan that I have explained and thus bring on the crisis," said Eina.

"I see. I see. Uv co'se yer wouldn't want me. I is er ill-littered man an' couldn't hardly be 'spected ter bring de crisis ter yer all ez I wouldn't know it ef I seed it. I ain't nevah seed one."

Eina and Clotille smiled at Uncle Jack's conception of a crisis, while Clotille said, "Well, you would be very likely to know this crisis when it came, Uncle Jack. And you are the very man that we have decided upon."

Uncle Jack lifted his head back, opened wide his eyes, while his jaws fell slightly apart. This serious piece of business was indeed a surprise to him.

"Yer ladies jes' wait heah er few minutes an' I'll come back an' give yer er answer."

So saying, Uncle Jack arose and slowly left the room, his frame having lost its erect carriage.

After a short stay in the stable, where he had stood with bowed head and folded arms, reflecting, Uncle Jack returned to the room where Eina and Clotille sat awaiting him.

"Fur yer ladies ter understan' de feelin's dat I been goin' through since yer all tole me whut yer wanted," began Uncle Jack, "I'll hab ter tell yer er leetul 'sperunce uv mine dat I had durin' uv de war.

"One day w'en de war wuz 'bout at its wust, I wuz goin' through de woods wid er gun an' two bird dogs. One uv dem dogs wuz name Abe Linktum an' de udder Jeff Davis. One uv 'um wuz fatten t'other an' I had ter be on my p's an' q's ter keep outen trouble. Yer see bofe Yankees an' 'federates wuz er roun' our country. W'en er 'federate come up ter me an' axt me de name uv de dogs, I allus pinted ter de fat dog an' say his name wuz Jeff Davis, an' ter de pore one an' say his name wuz Abe Linktum. W'en I would meet

Yankees an' dey would ax me I'd jes' turn it er roun' and de fat one would be Abe and de pore one Jeff.

"Dem pore dogs names wuz changed so much I dunno wedder dey knowed deyself whut wuz dare names."

"Hah, hah, hah," laughed Uncle Jack, memory of his shrewdness lighting up his dark face.

"But wunst I wuz in er jam, shuah 'nough. Some Yankees wanted one uv my dogs one day, an' says ter me, 'which one uv dem dogs is de bes'? Yer see ef I said Jeff, which wuz de pore one, under de succumstances, dey mought say, 'Ugh, huh, yer give Jeff Davis' name to de *bes'* dog? Yer see day mought not 'uve 'scused me fur namin' de bes' dog Jeff even ef he wuz de pore dog. Ef I said Abe wuz de bes', he bein' bofe bes' an' fat, dey would er shuah tuk him. So dare I wuz. I didun't hab no time ter think, but it jes' popped inter me whut ter say.

"I said, 'Gemmen, ter tell yer de truf, ain't nare one uv dem dogs much ercount. Darn um, bofe uv 'um sucks eggs.' Hah, hah, hah; dat got 'um.

"Now, it hez jes' allus been my way ter try ter fin' some kinder how ter git er long wid de white folks 'dout fussin' wid 'um. Whut yer all air sirgestin' is er long er leetul diffunt line, an' er feller had ter ketch his breath er leetul. Now, I doan' know ez yer all ketch on ter whut I is tryin' ter say. I says ergin, ladies, it wuz jes' er new line.

"But I 'spose times hab changed an' ez er cullud race we mus' stan' up now an' meet de diffunt qusshuns face ter face, face ter face. Wal, you young uns is able ter do dat. We ole uns wuz ignerrunt an' we jes' bowed an' scraped our way through ez bes' we could, 'tell yer all could git sense ernough ter make er bettah stan'.

"Sink er swim, keep er live er die, ez de poet says, I am wid yer ladies. But 'fore I starts out on dat mission I jes' mus' hab er vacation. W'en dat is ovah, yer goin' ter see yer Unce Jack comin' right back ter take up de cross yer young uns hez purpared fur him. Uncle Jack ain't feered. Nevah run frum nutthin' but er sperrit er ghost er sumpin' lak dat since I been bawn ter die."

CHAPTER XX.

FUNERAL OF A LIVE MAN.

FROM day to day Uncle Jack watched the movement of the sun as to its setting, noted the shortening of the days, the browning of the leaves upon the trees, and finally their falling to the earth.

"Wal, de persimmons is erbout right now an' de possums am fat, an' I s'pose its erbout time ter go."

Securing some one to fill his place for a short while, Uncle Jack now took his departure, omitting to state to any one where he was going or for what purpose.

A short distance from the side of the roadway bisecting Nelson County into eastern and western halves, sitting at the end of an archway several hundred feet long, which archway was made by two rows of well developed cedar trees, sat a somewhat large country farm-house. Uncle Jack with some difficulty opened the large farm gate.

"Times shuah doos change," said he, regaining his breath after his effort. "How well do I 'member how I uster fling dat gate open w'en I wuz er lad."

The old man looked wistfully down the tree made lane towards the house as he journeyed in that direction. His mind was on the spirits of the departed who once occupied the old house but were now gone forever. Arriving at the front door he started to knock, but changed his mind and went around to the rear.

"I'll go in at de back door ez I did in ole times."

In response to a knock on the rear door a small boy, followed by a bevy of open-mouthed children, alive with curiosity, opened the door and admitted Uncle Jack.

" 'Pon my soul ef it ain't old Jack Morris," said an aged woman, sitting near the fire blazing in the open fireplace, who had adjusted her spectacles and lifted her pipe from her mouth in order that she might the better survey the new-comer.

The name that the woman called brought the whole army of children about Uncle Jack's legs. In the home of his Aunt Melissa Crutcher and her son the name of Jack Morris was a household word, for Jack was the son of her brother, and as a youth had been uniformly kind to all and was dearly beloved by all, both white and black.

"Jack Morris, yer mean thing, yer, set down dare an' let me look at yer," said Aunt Melissa.

Uncle Jack did as he was bidden, and he and Aunt Melissa were soon exchanging reminiscences of old times.

By and by Horace Crutcher, Aunt Melissa's son, and Uncle Jack's cousin, who was now the owner of the old plantation on which Uncle Jack was a slave, came in, and was no less delighted than the others at the presence of Uncle Jack.

"Wal, yer all wants ter know what I'se heah fur, don't yer?" said Uncle Jack.

"Yer orter be heah ter lib tell yer die, Jack," said Aunt Melissa.

"Wal, I'se come ter be er man uv some 'portance in my ole days. I'm tole by some whut knows dat dare is er place cut out in der hist'ries fur me an' I mus' look atter dat putty soon. But I'se heah now ter hab er good ole time in ev'ry way, an' den ter hab my funeril preached."

"Your funeral preached?" asked Horace, Aunt Melissa's son.

"Yes, dat is whut I wants. I wants ter hab er good ole-fashion shout at de meetin' house; I wants er fust-class possum dinnah atter er all night hunt fur de possum, an' den, at er time w'en I kin hab all uv my frien's, white an' cullud, dat knowed me in de ole times, I wants my funeril preached."

At first it was thought that Uncle Jack was jesting, but it was finally seen that he was in earnest, and plans were set on foot to humor him in all his requests. The Crutcher boys were glad to lead him out one moonlight night in quest of the possums, and they and Uncle Jack were a delighted set when at daybreak next morning they returned with the coveted animals. Aunt Melissa Crutcher had stepped aside some years since for her daughter-in-law as a cook, but in this instance she bade her step aside and herself cooked the possum for Uncle Jack.

Sunday came, the church members were out in force and engaged in covenant meeting, the telling on the part of each of his christian experience and determination. Religious fervor ran high, the old plantation melodies were sung with zest, and a high degree of emotion was generated. Uncle Jack wept and laughed by turns from sheer joy, frequently exclaiming, "My soul is habin' er feast uv good things."

The funeral was duly announced, and on the appointed day the people, white and colored, dropped their tasks and met at the Negro church, where both the white and Negro pastors delivered eulogies concerning the white-haired Uncle Jack, who sat with bowed head in a corner of a front seat.

When the funeral was over and his life had been duly set forth to the hearers, the entire audience passed around and shook Uncle Jack by the hand.

When Uncle Jack had returned to Aunt Melissa's from the church, she said:

"Now, Jack Morris, yer air 'bout ter go back ter Belrose, an' I wouldn't lak ter die thinkin' dat Jack had turnt ter er fool. Now 'splain ter me dese goin' ons dat yer's been havin' out heah."

"Wal, Aunt Merlissa, ef you will sen' de chillun out I will 'splain things ter yer."

Aunt Melissa did as suggested, and Uncle Jack drew near so that he would not have to talk very loudly.

"Yer see, Aunt Merlissa, my way and yer way uv managin' wid de white folks wuz to act kin' an' make out wid de bes' dat dey seed fit ter do. I hez fell in wid some youngsters in Belrose dat wants things ter move 'cordin' ter some principull, an' not jes' ez er notion stracks de white people. Dey says dat de white people hez done gone an' disfrankshied ill-littered cullud folks 'thout disfrankshieng ill-littered white folks. Dese cullud young uns says dat ain't right. Dey says dat ill-littered white folks an' ill-littered cullud folks ought ter hab one law 'cordin' ter de constertution.

"Now I'se been picked out ez de cullud man ter tes' dat law. 'Fore I 'gin my life uv buckin' ergin er law uv de white folks I jes' wanted ter close up de life I *had* been livin', squar' an' even. Ef I had waited till I bucked de law de white folks mout not 'uve been willin' ter say all dis dey done said ovah me ter day.

"Yer see, dey ain't lak us. W'en massa rode erway ter de war an' fit ter keep me in slav'ry I didun't make it er pussonul mattah. I didun't lak whut he did, but I kep' on lakin' *him* jes' de same. I hopes de white folks won't git mad at me fur tryin' ter git er ekal show in life fur a cullud an' er white boy. But ef dey doos git mad, dey done 'spressed deyself 'bout my charackter."

CHAPTER XXI.

THE BREAK.

FOR sometime Miss Letitia Gilbreath had not been altogether pleased with the amount of attention that Baug was giving to Clotille. She noted that his visits were fewer by far than what they had been, and that when he did come his stay was invariably shorter than formerly. She observed also that Baug no longer accompanied Clotille to public affairs, leaving her to go with some girl friend.

Miss Letitia decided to constitute herself a detective to find out just what the trouble was. She was not long in discovering why Baug was not oftener at Clotille's house. It was simply because he was giving his entire attention socially to one Miss Eina Rapona.

When Miss Letitia caught sight of the beautiful Eina, her heart somewhat sank within her. She realized that, after all, there was a possible basis for a marked affinity between people of a similar mould, and that the small fraction of the blood of the colored race possessed by each made an attachment between Eina and Baug more probable, perhaps, than between the light Baug and the dark Clotille. Against most girls Clotille, she felt, had the advantage of a large prospective fortune, but she discovered that Eina was also a girl of wealth.

Miss Letitia tried to arouse Clotille's fears of losing Baug that she might bestir herself to hold his affections, but Clotille was only too happy that Eina had him in tow and was hauling him out of her way; as for the rest of her problem she was now convinced that with Belrose all right, with the permanence of the Belrose movement assured, with unequal disfranchisement destined to be upset, her cousin could be handled. So, that which was bringing worry to Miss Letitia was bringing happiness to Clotille.

Unable to arouse Clotille to action in her own behalf, Miss Letitia decided to take up the cudgel herself and drive Eina from the field. At a time when Clotille was away from home she opened her letter box and purloined what she regarded as ample ammunition with which to attack Eina.

Mounting her bicycle, Miss Letitia rode out to where she had learned that Eina lived. As soon as she had taken a seat in Eina's parlor she plunged into the object of her visit.

"You and my Clotille are fast friends, I believe?" said Miss Letitia.

"We surely are," said Eina, her face aglow with the thought of the mutual love between herself and Clotille.

"Yes, I think you are. I know that, being a friend, you would not have her live and die a pauper," said Miss Letitia.

"Of course not. I would do all in my power to see Clotille's life full of comfort," said Eina.

"I felt that way about you. And I knew that the harm you were doing Clotille was being done because you did not understand just what was taking place."

"Indeed, you speak the truth when you say that I am in ignorance concerning any form of injury that I am doing Clotille. And pray please be frank and quick. It pains me to have so acted at any time or place as to have impressed any one that Clotille's interests needed protection from my aggression," said Eina, rising and moving toward Miss Letitia in her eagerness to catch her every word.

"Well, Clotille stands a good chance of being rich some day, but it all depends upon whom she marries. A respectable fortune awaits her if she marries Baug Peppers."

"Who?" shouted Eina.

"Baug Peppers," slowly repeated Miss Letitia.

Eina's head grew dizzy, a weakness seized every muscle of her frame, and she staggered to the nearest chair and fell into it. Up to that moment she had never in her life known what the depth of love was nor realized how madly she was in love with Peppers. Her throat was dry, her lips parched and her frame all a quiver.

"Yes," continued Miss Letitia, "Baug and Clotille have been picked out for each other for years and years."

"She did not tell me, she did not tell me," Eina at last found strength to say.

"Well, Clotille was always backwards about her rights; but I am telling you."

"Conroe?"

"I'll see her in her grave before I'll let her marry that fellow," said Miss Letitia.

"Does she love Baug?" asked Eina.

"They love each other," said Miss Letitia.

Eina now rallied and said: "Miss Gilbreath, Clotille is my friend, my only, my dearest friend. If she had loved Baug Peppers she would have let me know. You are in error, somehow. Clotille would not; Clotille, *Clotille* could not play me false."

Miss Letitia now unfolded a little package which she had kept in her hand, saying, "You know Clotille's handwriting. Read this letter, will you? Notice the date, too, won't you?"

Eina took the letter into her trembling hands and saw at once that it was unmistakably written in Clotille's hand.

It was addressed to "My own dear Baug," breathed throughout the most fervent love, and was evidently written in response to a letter of the same tenor that Clotille had received. There at the close of the letter were penned these significant words:

"Though our ambitions may cause us to not be seen in each other's company, you know me and I know you. You are my Baug and I know nothing in all the world other than to subscribe myself here and hereafter, your CLOTILLE."

Eina's mind now flashed back to Baug's standing on Broadway and Seventh Avenue the day of her arrival, to Clotille's significant laugh. It all now looked to her to be a black, black conspiracy to foster some secret ambition that Baug and Clotille cherished, for the attainment of which she had apparently been made a tool.

"Brood of vipers, I drive you from my heart," said Eina.

"Woman, please leave my house. Never fear that I shall stand between Clotille and that man. Please go," cried Eina.

Miss Letitia arose to leave, and on departing, glanced a last time into Eina's face. Never in all her life had she seen such a picture of woe as she now left behind her, but it moved her not.

Eina collapsed the moment Miss Letitia left, and for a long while lay prone on the floor. At length she crawled to her desk and penned the following note to Baug:

"Baug Peppers: The engagement for this evening is off. Please do not ever again call at my house.

EINA RAPONA."

Having dispatched this note, Eina, in an aimless manner, wandered from room to room in her cottage, alternately wringing her hands and holding them to her throbbing temples.

"Is life worth living?"

Such was the question that the sad, torn heart of Eina now asked over and over again.

"I was young and wealthy and the world called me beautiful."

"I lived in Boston and no door was closed in my face. I met a colored girl, and the colored blood in me called out unto her, and we became friends."

* * * *

"For her sake I left my home, came to the land of the great shadow, the land of the great shadow, the land of the great shadow, and cast my lot with her."

* * * *

"Her burdens were my burdens, and I threw my soul into the work of clearing the pathway of life for her. She deliberately interests me in a man with whom she was herself in love, while pretending to love another."

* * * *

"She puts near me a trusted servant who would be sure to bring this man into my life. I can see it all now, all! I meet him, I work with him, I—I—I—well, here I am, a broken-hearted girl. Faith—in—humanity gone, gone; all gone."

* * * *

"What is there in life when the heart is bleak? Money I have, but what is that as a solace to the spirit?"

* * * *

"The world is large, but what of it if your heart is chained to the one spot?"

* * * *

"I am young yet, but more is the pity, for the longer will I have this load to carry. Oh life, what are you? Just as we reach out our hands to clutch you, you go."

* * * *

"What is the moon that we call so beautiful? A dried-up land. What is the sun? A ball of fire that we dare not approach."

* * * *

"Where are our ancestors? In us, for we eat their dust."

* * * *

"What was the fate of the one true man that came into the world? Crucified."

* * * *

"Whence came I? Who knoweth?"

* * * *

"Whither goeth man after death? Who hath returned to tell?"

* * * *

"Is life worth living? Is death any better?"

* * * *

"The path—of—glory—leads but—to—the grave."

CHAPTER XXII.

LIGHT COMES.

WHEN Baug Peppers received that little note, unmistakably penned by Eina, he rushed pellmell to a livery stable, called for and hired the fastest horse therein, and went dashing toward Eina's home as fast as the fleet animal could carry him. When, at the end of what had seemed to be an age, he came to Eina's house, he found the blinds closed, the doors barred and no one to respond to his repeated knockings.

Finding all efforts to get in touch with Eina futile, Baug rushed around the house to the stable in quest of Uncle Jack.

He read the note to Uncle Jack and asked him what on earth could possibly be the trouble.

"Wal, I been 'spectin' jes' dis," said Uncle Jack, deliberately.

"Expecting it?" roared Baug.

"Expecting Miss Rapona to deny me the privilege of seeing her? Why, her request is just about as reasonable as though she asked me not to breathe! And you have been expecting it?" stormed Baug.

"Be ca'm, Baug; be ca'm an' heah me. Be ca'm! Be ca'm!"

"Uncle, if you are going to talk, please talk in keeping with the fitness of things. Don't, don't say be ca'm. There is a far more appropriate *be* that could be said by a less devout man that would better fit this occasion—*no, no,* that thought is wicked, and I need heaven's help right now," said Baug.

"Yer see, Baug, de lady keers fur yer."

"Uncle Jack, dear Uncle Jack, I love you, but you *lie*. You say *I* see that the lady cares for me. That is exactly what I don't see."

"Baug, lak my white folks, I doan' take de lie frum nobody, but bein's yer is crazy, I'll take it ter day. Yer 'minds me uv—"

"Uncle Jack, I'll murder you on the spot—no, I love you too much for that, but I will say I will never forgive you if you try to joke me now," said Baug, tramping around impatiently, his eye roving about the doors and windows of Eina's home, hoping to catch a glimpse of her.

"Yer see, Baug, de lady hez come ter de conclusion dat she mus' know mo' 'bout yer 'fo' proceedin' furder wid yer. W'en er 'oman takes dat co'se she's gittin' mighty deep in love. Things air putty bright fur yer, old boy, putty bright."

"If things are bright now, I hope to heaven to *never, never* see them dark," said Baug.

"Yer see, findin' dat she laks yer, she mus' now wait 'till she kin git yer pedigrees, kin fin' out whar yer sprung frum," said Uncle Jack.

"Oh, my stars! Then I am gone! Who on earth knows where I came from? That has been the one shadow on my soul. I can't blame the girl if that's the case. How do I know but what my father was hanged? Oh, I am done forever," said Baug, growing even more alarmed, if that be possible, and ploughing his hand through his hair frantically.

"But now I may be barkin' up de wrong tree, sumpin' else maybe de mattah; yer had bettah go see Miss Clotille, bettah see her," said Uncle Jack, gravely.

Baug acted on the suggestion, and was soon on the way to Clotille's house.

When the news of Eina's attitude toward Baug reached Clotille through the latter, Clotille was both amazed and alarmed.

Clotille and Baug now gave earnest thought to the devising of some plan for finding out at once what was the cause of all the trouble. They were engaged in an earnest whispered conversation, and Miss Letitia was sure that they were at last planning for their wedding.

Feeling that there was danger in delay, Miss Letitia concluded to help bring matters to a head that very day.

Entering the parlor where Baug and Clotille were, she said:

"Children, it rejoices my heart to see you two so loving."

Clotille looked up to see if there were any indications of her cousin's losing her mind.

"Yes, I think you all were born for each other, Baug handsome and intelligent, Clotille pretty, talented and cultured, and in sight and in reach of a great fortune whenever she fulfills the conditions."

"Oh, Cousin Letitia, that is horrid, horrid! Pray what on earth is the matter?" said Clotille.

"No, I am going to speak my mind to-day. The reason things came so near going wrong was because I kept my mouth closed so long. Young people need to be guided. You two would not have been together so long and lovingly to-day if I had not knocked the other one off of the track. I did not want to do it, but she had no right to come between you two and upset all our plans."

A faint glimmer of the true state of affairs dawned upon Clotille and Baug, and they both stood up looking eagerly to Miss Letitia for more light.

"Now that looks nice. You all will make a nice couple, a light one and a dark one. Now let the other lady get a dark one," said Miss Letitia.

"To—I'll cut any dark one's throat—I don't understand," said Baug.

"I have just told her that you and Clotille were picked out for each other a long time ago."

"Mercy! Mercy!" screamed Clotille.

"She was hard to shake, but I shook her. I found some letters that Baug returned to you when you all evidently broke up, and I showed her one of them. That letter settled things and she will never give you two any more trouble. You young people must watch these designing women now and hereafter else they will ruin you," continued Miss Letitia.

"Oh, woman, in what a perfidious light you have placed me. Now let me tell you something. For years I have loved a dark man, Conroe Driscoll. Because you have fought with such bitterness my marrying a dark man, he has used Baug's name in his correspondence so that a discovery of his letters on your part would not give us trouble. When Conroe grew somewhat hopeless and didn't care whether he lived or died on the football field, he returned to me my letters to him that they might not fall into other hands in case of his death. It was evidently a letter of mine to Conroe which you found and used."

CHAPTER XXIII.

QUITE UNEXPECTED.

BAUG stood listening to what Clotille and Miss Letitia had to say long enough to catch a clear idea of what caused his trouble, and then, with all the speed at his command, hastened to his buggy and was soon at Eina's home again, but his success at getting a hearing was no better this time than on his previous visit, and he drove back dejectedly to Clotille, who was still weeping bitterly over the false light in which her cousin had put her.

"Come, Baug, I will settle it all," said Clotille, rising and leading the way to the buggy.

"Drive me quickly to Conroe's office."

Baug obeyed, not knowing, however, what was Clotille's plan.

When they arrived at the office Clotille said: "Conroe, go at once and get a marriage license."

Conroe hesitated an instant and looked into Baug's face for an explanation.

"Yes, for God's sake, go, and go quickly!"

Conroe not daring to hope that the sun had come to shine in his door, took it for granted that it was Baug who was to be thus favored of heaven. Therefore upon arriving at the office where licenses were issued, he procured a license for Baug Peppers and Eina Rapona. He returned to his office, where he found that a justice of the peace, summoned during his absence, awaited to perform a marriage ceremony.

Conroe handed the license to the justice, and Clotille said, "We are ready."

"But where, where—er—I don't understand. Where is Miss Rapona?" asked Conroe.

"You fool you, you and Clotille are to marry, Conroe," shouted Baug.

Slowly it percolated through Conroe's brain that he and not Baug was the fortunate mortal and out of the office he dashed for another license. In the meantime Baug made himself the possessor of the license that Conroe had mistakenly procured, and surreptitiously slipped the paper into his pocket, not knowing what strange turn events might take that day, and desiring to be prepared not only for the worst but also for the best.

It was remarkable how much quicker Conroe made the second trip to the license office than he did the first, although he would have testified on oath that his first trip was made with as much speed as was consistent with dignity. But you see in his own case he abandoned all considerations of dignity.

Soon Conroe Driscoll and Clotille Strange were proclaimed man and wife.

"Let us all go to see Eina now and take this justice along as a witness," said Clotille.

The suggestion was accepted and the party procured a carriage, which ere long pulled up to

Eina's gate. Clotille rushed to the house, leaving the others behind, hoping to prepare the way for them. It happened that she had retained the key to Eina's door that she had when in charge of the preparations for Eina's coming, and had been thoughtful enough to get it before leaving home.

She opened the door and rushed in. But Eina had gone!

CHAPTER XXIV.

BAUG SEARCHING FOR EINA.

CONROE DRISCOLL and Baug Peppers are in absolute disagreement as to the character of the first night after Eina's disappearance. Happy in the possession of Clotille as his bride, Conroe positively asserts that the world was never more beautiful than on that night. According to his account, the moon was full and in jovial mood. The clouds to vex her reign were thin and few, and even they, in passing beneath her throne, were tinged with glory and made resplendent in the heavens. The milky way, like a diamond studded bridal veil, hovered near the moon as if to be in easy reach of this beautiful woman of the night traveling toward some consort divine. The stars, both great and small, twinkled their merriest as if in an effort to keep pace with their happy queen. Now this is Conroe's version of that night, set forth according to the emotions that surged within him as he stood out in the open and thanked the far off eternal forces which, despite all obstacles, had swept Clotille into his arms.

As for Baug, he vehemently asserts that the light of the moon was wearisome to the soul; that the winking and blinking stars were but so many tiny mockers of his grief; that all of nature's antics on that night were out of keeping with the eternal fitness of things save where the dark shadows and sullen corners were to be found, where the light of the moon and stars came not.

It is perhaps the discontented man of the world that bears watching, so we shall for the time being excuse ourselves from the company of the happy Conroe and follow the meanderings of the rather desperate Baug.

Without set purpose, Baug left his gate that night and began to walk aimlessly through the streets of Belrose. Passing through the heart of the city, moving in an opposite direction to that in which Eina had lived, Baug walked far beyond the corporate limits, his journeyings bringing him to the Ambrose River, leisurely flowing along, fresh from lapping the shores of Belrose.

Upon the bridge spanning the river, Baug looked down upon the sombre face of the waters, then toward the gloom-steeped trees lining the banks of the stream, then toward the hills that rose in the distance and seemed to bank themselves against the sky. Returning his gaze to the waters, Baug said:

"Dark, wooing waters, one day your smileless face may draw me to your bosom, but not now, not now! I have a great battle to fight—and win. To live, to live, and not to die, is my task."

When, far across the river, Baug, following the roadway, reached the crest of a high hill and saw near the roadside a huge boulder, he paused, climbed upon the rock and sat with his face toward sleeping Belrose, determined to abide there until he had worked out some satisfactory plan for searching for the missing Eina.

What made the situation doubly agonizing to Baug was the fact that Eina, according to Uncle Jack, had resolved to die to the Negro race.

"If that girl passes for white, what a terrible situation confronts me! As a colored man I never attend their churches, theatres, or social gatherings, nor they ours. We are two distinct worlds meeting in business relations through the day and retiring within our respective racial castles at night. If on the streets of Belrose I happen to meet Eina and accost her socially while she is passing for white, any crowd of white Belrosans seeing it will be ready to mob me. Terrible, terrible, terrible predicament," mused Baug.

"If I should pass for white and make the search for Eina in the social circles of the whites, and perchance should be discovered, death would assuredly await me, though my heart would only be in quest of Eina," he continued. Then the thought occurred to him that his face of mystery, having always attracted the marked attention of all who had met him, would perhaps be in the way of such a course.

As a sort of rest from the strain of trying to decide upon a line of procedure, Baug's mind now reverted to his various talks with Eina, and there came back to him to both gladden and to further sadden his heart, Eina's sunny smile, the glory of her eyes, the memory of the thrill of her low, sweet tones, the noble sentiments to which from time to time she had given voice.

As Baug sat thus meditating on his seemingly hopeless plight, glancing down the road he saw in the moonlight the dim outline of a human form. It proved to be that of the ever-faithful Uncle Jack, who, knowing the intensity of Baug's attachment for Eina, had felt that it was at least well to keep in touch with him.

From the moment that he had caught sight of the look of desperation that overspread Baug's face when he had intimated to him Eina's determination to withdraw from the Negro race, Uncle Jack had been on Baug's trail, managing, however, to keep at such a distance as to be unobserved. During the time that he had been following Baug, Uncle Jack had been canvassing in his mind a matter of deep moment. He knew that the ruling desire of Baug's heart now was to find Eina, and he felt able to indicate the manner in which this might be done, but the carrying out of his plan might jeopardize his own life. In view of this possible danger he had thought long and deeply.

Having at last reached a conclusion, Uncle Jack emerged from the shadow of the trees by the roadside where he had stopped to rest and keep watch on Baug. As he drew near, Baug, whose soul just now craved solitude, for the first time in life was not glad to see him. Many a time had Baug in days gone by sought Uncle Jack in order that he might dispel feelings of gloom by drawing on his rich store of humorous experiences, but at this time he felt more like listening to a funeral discourse than to a joke. Uncle Jack, however, very soon turned Baug's distaste at his presence into unbounded joy.

In a tone that smacked of impatience, Baug said: "Uncle Jack, what on earth has brought you way out here at such a time as this. A man of your years should take better care of himself."

Uncle Jack, knowing Baug's frame of mind, elected to ignore the tone of irritation, and said in an humble manner:

"Baug, Miss Eina is done gone, ez yer knows, an' I wants ter fin' her. 'Cordin' ter whut I learns she lef' under er misunderstandin'."

"Yes, a very, very gross one, Uncle Jack. The idea of her supposing that Clotille was in love with me and I with Clotille!"

"Now, I wants ter fin' Miss Eina an' git all dis cleared up."

"Of course everybody wants to find her, Uncle Jack. But how in the name of common sense is that to be done is the question?"

"Now dat is whut I wants ter talk wid yer erbout. I got er plan dat will shuah bring her ter whar yer kin 'splain matters ter her."

Baug leaped down from his boulder, slapped Uncle Jack upon the shoulder and said: "Uncle

Jack, you are the very man I'm looking for. Upon my word and honor I would rather have your company than to own a South African gold mine. Now out with your plan, Uncle Jack."

"Did yer evah talk ter Miss Eina 'bout de cullud folks bein' disfrankshied?"

Baug's mind became very alert and very exact, very much disposed to dwell on details. How baffiled love does sharpen one's wits! Said he:

"Oh, yes, many a time. Let's see. I think I can almost recall the words in which I expressed my views on that. I said to her something like this: Governments have a psychological influence over their citizens. The reverence which makes a government possible writes itself large upon the citizen's mind, who often unconsciously seeks to reflect in himself the spirit of his State. Wherever, therefore, you find a State discriminating against a given class, the citizen assumes a like attitude toward the object of discrimination in an effort to reflect the attitude of the State. In the very nature of things, therefore, matters, where State action is one great fountain of psychological poison, must grow worse instead of better. Yes, State discrimination is a virus calculated to carry unfairness into the very marrow and bone of the nation."

"Wal, whut yer said made er deep 'pression on her mind an' she got all wrapped up in takin' dat qusshun ter de S'preme Coat. She wuz plannin' er case 'thout yer knowin' it, ter tes' de law. Yer wuz ter be kep' out uv de plannin' so dat yer woulden't be 'rested for cunspeericy, fur she wanted yer fur de lawyer."

"Oh, bosh, Uncle Jack! I thought you had a plan for finding Miss Eina?"

"Jes' hole yer hosses, Mistah Baug; jes' hole yer hosses, an' doan' be so ready ter fly off," said Uncle Jack, reassuringly.

"Miss Eina kinder thort yer wuz er great man an' she wanted ter heah yer argify dat case in de S'preme Coat. She said dat ef dat case wuz evah called up dare she would be dare ef she lived. She said dat ef she wuz dead an' dare wuz enny such thing ez er dead pusson visitin' 'bout, she would shuah be dare. Now, Baug, Uncle Jack knows folks—white folks, cullud folks an' de mixed folks. Uncle Jack knows 'um. I tell yer shuah ez yer is bawn, ef yer git er case in de S'preme Coat to tes' dem disfrankshieing laws, Miss Eina will be on han' ter hear yer argify. Baug, I tell yer I knows."

"Now, Uncle Jack," said Baug, enthusiastically, "you go ahead with that test case, you hear. Do everything just as you were told by Miss Eina. Keep me way out of the thing, if telling me will keep me from being the attorney. Do you hear, Uncle Jack?"

With this line of procedure agreed upon, the two men sat throughout the night chatting, Baug listening with hungry ears to little scraps of remarks that Eina had from time to time let fall in Uncle Jack's presence, remarks indicating that she took more than a passing interest in him. More than once Uncle Jack was in imminent danger of being hugged by Baug over some remark of Eina's that he reported.

By and by the moon went down, the east took on its golden flush and the hazy light of morning appeared. Vehicles began to pass, and when one came along that afforded an opportunity for a ride, Baug accosted the driver, who readily consented to convey him and Uncle Jack to Belrose.

CHAPTER XXV.

CLEAR SAILING.

WHILE Baug was fully resolved upon carrying out the plan that Uncle Jack had laid before him there was the possibility of ill effects that he desired if possible to avoid. He realized fully that the good will of his Southern white neighbors was a consideration second only in importance to having it agreed that the race with which he was identified was to be dealt with according to the fundamental principle of the government, equality before the law. He had inaugurated in Belrose the harmonious working together of the white and colored people in local political matters, and he would have regretted much anything that rendered him personally unacceptable as an ambassador of peace.

Of course he had all along been deeply concerned about the fundamental rights of his people, was anxious to have the point that had so greatly interested Eina settled, but he had hitherto hoped that that possibly irritating duty might fall to some other hands; had hoped this, not out of cowardice, but from a desire to reserve himself for a task of equal importance, that of friendly adjustment.

Moreover Baug felt that an attempt on his part to overthrow even by peaceable means what he deemed the unequal suffrage system might jeopardize his life. As he desired above all things just now to live to see Eina again he thought it wise to sound Molair that he might indirectly gain an idea as to whether it was best to prosecute his work in this direction from some point in the North or from Belrose.

Calling upon Mr. Molair at his home after business hours were over, Baug was ushered into his library. When Molair entered he greeted Baug with a smile and a warm clasp of the hand.

Beginning the conversation, Baug said:

"Mr. Molair, I regard you as typical of the best that Southern white civilization has produced, and through you I want to-day to hear the voice of the best South."

"I thank you for your compliment, but I dare not claim to be the best of the South, which, Southerner-like, I put ahead of the world. You see the heights are too dizzy," replied Molair.

Passing by Molair's parrying of his compliment, Baug said: "I am more than anxious that the political war along racial lines between your and my people should come to a close, and would regret the necessity of any step that would put us more at variance. But the vital needs of the colored people, with which needs my own personal fortunes have become inextricably involved, demand that I make an effect to have our Supreme Court upset such laws as do not bear equally upon the people of both races. In the event that I pursue this course what do you think would be the attitude of the Southern white people of your type?"

Molair smiled and cast his eyes around the walls of the library. Arising, he went to the end of a row of oil paintings of persons, and said to Baug: "Come and look." He lead Baug from painting to painting in that room, then escorted him to other rooms where there were paintings. When the tour of inspection was over, he said: "You have just seen the likenesses of Molairs for centuries back. So far as I am concerned, if with a thousand years of civilization back of him a Molair cannot hold his own in an equal contest with the grandson of an uncivilized African, I say let him go to the wall. I scorn the idea of a weak test for a white man and a severe one for the Negro. It is a rank injustice to the white man. When your remember that mother nature coddled, made life easy for Africa, but was stern and penurious with England, you can see the danger that will come to the Southern white man if we indulge him while making exactions of the Negro.

"The sooner the standard of voting for the white man is made as high as that for the colored man, the better for the white man. Indulgence leads to decay, not to advancement," said Molair, his whole attitude signifying abhorrence of the notion of coddling any section of the white race.

"I am glad to hear you speak thus, Mr. Molair. In the event that my course is questioned, I trust that you will give voice to such sentiments as you have just expressed."

The interview now came to a close, and Baug took his departure with a much lighter heart. With great zest he entered upon the task of raising the funds necessary to fight through the test case to be inaugurated by Uncle Jack according to secret plans laid out by Eina.

Baug withheld action on Uncle Jack's part looking toward the testing of the law in question until such a time as he should feel able to take care of the financial end of the matter.

Ah, that was a dreary, dreary wait! And while Baug in thus waiting, and chafing while he waits, let us take advantage of the opportunity to catch a glimpse of other friends of ours.

CHAPTER XXVI.

DESIRES HER WILL CHANGED.

IF the marriage of Clotille and Conroe could have been postponed until Baug was disposed of, and until the conception had been fully developed in Miss Letitia's mind that the harmonious relations between the races in Belrose were to continue, it might have been that the wedding would not have so excited the wrath of Miss Letitia; but as it was, her rage was boundless. When on the day following her marriage, Clotille returned to her cousin's home for the purpose of pleading her cause, Miss Letitia slammed the door in her face. As for Conroe, she despised him utterly.

"The black varmint! I feel like wringing his old head off. The idea of him poking his old black face into our family!" Such was the comment Miss Letitia passed upon Conroe.

Having felt assured that Clotille would marry in a manner to please her, Miss Letitia had drawn up her will, leaving her fortune to her, but she now resolved upon changing all this, and proceeded at once to Seth Molair's office for the purpose of having him draw up another will.

"Well, what has the former beneficiary done to displease you, if I am not asking too much?" inquired Molair in an effort to draw Miss Letitia out, not being altogether pleased with that fanatical look in her eye.

"She has turned out to be a fool," snapped out the angry Miss Letitia.

"Gone mad?" asked Molair, in surprise.

"Worse than that."

"Oh," said Molair, afraid to pursue the subject any further, as it seemed to involve some moral turpitude.

"Yes, I would have rather seen her in her grave a thousand times than for her to have turned out like she did," said Miss Letitia.

"Too bad; too bad. But you can console yourself with the fact that you set her a good example and taught her the right way."

"I haven't set her any example at all. I am a *miss*. But I taught her the right way all right, the crazy thing."

"Oh, she is really crazy, then?" remarked Molair.

"Crazy? Of course she is crazy, as crazy as any lunatic in the asylum."

"Well, we ought to have her put up, then," said Molair.

"I wish you could send her to the penitentiary and hang the black ape."

Molair was considerably puzzled as to just what the nature of the case was, and he was disposed to drop the discussion, but Miss Letitia never tired of letting people know just what she thought of the matter.

"Yes, sir, as many yellow girls as that fellow could have got, and some of them almost white, too—the idea of him, as black as he is, marrying Clotille. It's a shame. It has almost broken my heart."

"Black as he is! Who in the thunder is this Clotille that you object to her marrying a black man? Is *she* white?" asked Molair.

"White! Of course not. There is where the outrage comes in. She is black. The idea of two black people marrying each other in America when they have got a chance to marry lighter!"

Molair now laid down his pen and looked intently at Miss Letitia, it beginning to dawn upon him as to what the true situation was.

"Do you mean to say that you are going to disinherit this dark girl because she has decided to marry a man with a complexion similar to her own?" asked Molair.

"That is exactly what I am going to do, sir. I shall cut her off without a penny. Who wants to always be a problem? Who wants some one else to always have his foot on your neck? America hasn't got enough of the grace of God in her heart to treat a black man as she would a white man. Her life is a living lie. And I want every drop of the despised blood sucked into her veins. I want her to eat up the race she hates. You have set the colored man's house on fire, you pour oil on it every day and keep it burning. Don't rats leave a sinking ship? Don't lice crawl off of the scalp of a dying person? Don't we bury corpses? Sure, I'll disinherit that girl for marrying so as to perpetuate the black face, the seed of discord. I'll cut her off without a copper and wish that I could will for her to beg bread from door to door, so help me Moses."

Molair reflected awhile and then said: "Now, I am a Southern white man, and believe in the preservation of both races. I do not care, even in a professional way, to be connected with your notion of the absorption of the blood of your race into ours."

"Aha! Aha!" said Miss Letitia, rising, "you disfranchise, you ostracize, you jim crow, you lynch, you burn a man because he is colored, then hold up your hands in holy horror because he seeks, by honorable means, to get away from being colored. If you want a man to stay colored, why in the name of God don't you treat him right as colored? That fool Clotille has gone back on me, but don't you forget the leaven is at work, and if you don't treat the colored people right in every way, in the ages to come, you are not going to have any colored people."

Drawing near to Molair, Miss Letitia pointed her finger at him and said: "You tell the Negro-hater among the whites to keep on building the fires of prejudice, keep on jim crowing Negroes, keep on disfranchising, keep on painting the sky as black as midnight! Aha, keep on! Millions have crossed into your race already and millions are to follow, yes millions are to follow. Put that in your pipe, great sir, and smoke it! We will all be white one day, and it won't be by intermarriage, either."

With her head thrown high in the air, Miss Gilbreath swept majestically out of Molair's office.

When Miss Letitia had gone, Molair sat with knitted brow toying with his pencil, giving earnest thought to the situation presented by her attitude.

"Indirect amalgamation is this woman's game, I see. But I want no amalgamation, direct or indirect, immediate or remote. I want no incorporation of the Negro blood into our race even after that blood has been so diluted as to lose its power of pigmentation. I don't want Negro blood in the blood of our race even though it be in the proportion to the waters of Lake Erie to those of the Atlantic and Pacific oceans combined." Such were Molair's thoughts as he contemplated Miss Letitia's course.

"Now what am I to do to balk this game? We toss all mulattoes to the Negroes. We cannot pass a law forbidding them to intermarry with the Negroes and forcing them to intermarry among themselves. And if we did force them to intermarry among themselves exclusively, would we not soon have a large white race of them ready for surreptitious disappearance into our ranks?" reflected Molair.

Reaching for his telephone Molair called up

the more prominent members of the Belrose bar and asked them as an act of professional courtesy to him to refuse to draw up a will for one Letitia Gilbreath, colored, who might call upon them for such service. Molair had divined that Miss Letitia was of that class of colored people of an aristocratic turn of mind, whose sympathies were with the more aristocratic element of whites, and he felt assured that she would not call upon the Negro attorneys nor the more humble white lawyers for service, but upon the white lawyers of eminence, locally. So correctly had he gauged Miss Letitia that she entered no law office but that his message had preceded her. Everywhere, therefore, she met with a polite but positive refusal to do the work that she desired done.

Thoroughly enraged, Miss Letitia returned to her home vowing that she would draw the will herself, and to that end began the purchase of law books, and the study of law. It was an interesting sight to behold her with her eye glasses sitting high upon her nose poring over authorities on wills.

"Yes, sir; I'll have me a will that will disinherit a Driscoll to the ten-thousandth generation and I won't consult them poor white lawyers nor the colored ones either. I'll draw the will myself if it takes me a lifetime to get it straight," was Miss Letitia's emphatic boast.

CHAPTER XXVII.

MOLAIR AT WORK.

THE more Molair reflected on the situation of Conroe and Clotille, as disclosed by his interview with Miss Letitia, the more he found his sympathies going out to them.

"Here," said Molair to himself, "is a test of my sincerity on this matter of preserving racial integrity. I must see to it that this couple does not lose by the course they have pursued and this woman must be converted, just *must* be. How can we hope to deal with this great question in the large if we can't handle it in small bits?"

Molair now entered upon a close study of Miss Letitia, not hesitating to call upon her and to engage her in close conversation, searching for the mainspring of the benumbing pessimism that held her within its grasp. Discovering incidentally what a great admiration Miss Letitia had for fire fighters, it occurred to Molair that it might be possible to have Conroe ingratiate himself into her good graces through service in this department.

The man at the head of the colored fire company, having had no previous experience in dealing with men as subordinates, was not giving entire satisfaction, and Mayor Molair, anxious that this initial experiment should prove to be eminently successful, had been casting about for a more competent man for a captain. Inquiry concerning

Conroe convinced Molair that he was a man of the type desired, so he sent for Conroe and made him a tender of the position.

To Conroe, Molair put the matter in the following light:

"We are inaugurating a new era in Belrose, and what we do here may spread over the South. The Negroes who honestly seek to work with us in a patriotic manner are to be encouraged. So much depends upon how we start off. I know that it will not pay you as well financially to be a captain of a fire department as to be a physician; nor in the eyes of the public will as much dignity attach to the post. But surely it is a cause well worthy of a sacrifice, the paving of the way for the utilization of members of your race in the public service."

Thus appealed to, Conroe gave up the promise of a successful medical career to take charge of the colored fire company. Clotille at first demurred, then thinking of what a splendid opportunity was thus afforded Conroe to win Miss Letitia's favor, she gave her assent. It was thus that Conroe entered the Belrose fire department.

And just as was expected, Conroe's stalwart figure fighting the flames from time to time appealed to the imagination of Miss Letitia, and her attitude toward him began to soften so that Clotille's hopes began to rise.

But in order that he might be able to present to the diseased mind of Miss Letitia overwhelming evidence that a brighter day was ahead, Molair decided to branch out in every needful direction where he had cause to think that he would effect a result that would serve as oil on the hinges of the door of hope. The one thing in the South that had caused Molair's heart to quake with fear because of the ocean of possibilities bound up in it, was the *"bad Negro"* element with its power to summon from their sleep long discarded savage instincts. Molair therefore now gave thought to this "bad Negro" question.

Thus one morning as the ministers of the colored churches of Belrose were in the midst of their weekly meeting in one of their church edifices, Molair unexpectedly put in his appearance. As white men now very rarely attended Negro meetings the coming of Molair was a genuine surprise.

As an act of courtesy to the Mayor, the suspension of the regular order was moved that the body might hear whatever the Mayor might have to say.

Molair went forward and said: "Members of the Conference, a matter of deep concern brings me to you this morning." On the faces of all there came the most intent expression as a result of this remark.

"What on earth can it be now?" was the thought of the colored men who, like the whites, were ever on the alert, always apprehensive as to what was to come next.

"Since I have been your Mayor I have been passing over Belrose, noting the condition of your people. Many, very many, of you are going up, up, up, and I am proud of this very evident progress. (Applause.)

"But side by side with this upward movement on the part of many, there is, I have observed, an appalling downward movement. Evidently hope and self-respect have broken loose in a number of your race and they are sinking, sinking to awful depths. Just think of what is called 'Hell's Half Acre,' and that settlement surrounding the building known as the 'Ark.' I doubt that, this side of the hell of which you preach, you will find such terrible degradation elsewhere."

"The slums of New York," a voice interposed.

"Yes, yes. But,— at any rate, let us keep our minds on Belrose just now." (Applause.)

"Now, as to how much my people, the Southern white people, have contributed to this degeneracy by tolerating things that smacked of hostility to your race, I have not come this morning to argue. Nor am I unmindful of the fact that a measure of the aloofness of your upper classes toward this decaying element is in part due, perhaps to the fact that it has been preached to them that the bad Negro keeps the good Negro back. Thus taught, the less spiritual among you have perhaps grown to hate your submerged fellows."

"That doctrine has had its effect," spoke up one.

"I have come here to assure you as the Mayor of Belrose that I shall stand for exact justice, the impartial enforcement of the law and the encouragement of all elements of our population to look upward and not downward. So now you good Negro Belrosans need not regard yourselves as having any personal problems because of your race, so far as I can remedy matters." (Prolonged applause.)

"Now, I have a favor to ask of you. You are going to find, I think, that the aspiring Negro will have much less of a problem concerning himself, so far as we whites are concerned. In this coming new day of hopefulness, nay, even before it is full upon you, can we not have you turn your thoughts, not away from your rights, but more toward these congested centers of vice, populated by your people? They breed disease, hold down real estate values, mar the beauty of our city, and they do you inestimable damage in the eyes of Northern visitors who are daily in our midst."

This last remark went home with great force. The maintaining of the respect and sympathy of the North, the author of freedom and enfranchisement, was a matter of deep concern to the Negroes, as Molair knew, and he had in him enough of the politician to pull on that chord for what he deemed a worthy purpose.

Continuing Mr. Molair said: "Is this not peculiarly your problem? Ties of blood link you to these denizens of an earthly hell. We may build a glorious structure here in Belrose, but from these depths can come the volcanic fires of evil in ferment that will overturn all that we create."

As a result of Molair's talk a meeting was arranged between the white and colored ministers and plans inaugurated for a vigorous crusade for the redemption of the centers of vice. Hopeful of the mitigation of this menace to the peace of both races, that in an evil moment might summon base passions that would overturn the work of ten thousand self-sacrificing lives, Molair now turned his thoughts in another direction.

CHAPTER XXVIII.

THE NORTH AND THE SOUTH.

RECOGNIZING the fact that the outside world, whether the South so willed or not, could by needlessly stirring up resentments within its borders, materially affect that wholesome atmosphere which he was now desirous of creating, Molair decided to accept an urgent invitation to a private interview which had been extended to him a short while back by the President of the United States, who had heard of the Belrose movement. With a view, therefore, to enlisting the President's co-operation in a policy that would aid him much in his work of atmosphere making, Molair took his journey to Washington and the White House.

"Mr. Molair, you have no idea of the profound satisfaction that we of the North have that a man of your type has caught hold of the outstretched hand of the better element of colored people," said the President, grasping Molair's hand warmly.

"Thank you, Mr. President," said Molair simply, preferring to have the President declare himself fully before having much to say himself.

"Now, I think that you people of the South have misunderstood me greatly as to my attitude toward the colored race, and I would like to lay bare my heart to you," said the President.

"I trust that you will, Mr. President. There should be the utmost candor in this matter."

"Well, to begin with, the great bulk of the colored people voted for me, their taxes help to pay my salary, and as Commander-in-Chief of the army and navy I bear a direct relation to their patriotism which is a part of our reliance for the defense of the flag."

"All very true," said Molair.

"I am a proud man, permit me to say, to this extent—I do not wish any man or set of men to do any more for me than I do for them. I do not like being, even to an infinitesimal extent, a pauper, living off of the unrequited bounty of others. As President, as the head of the nation, therefore, I have simply tried to give official recognition to this element of our population," said the President.

Continuing the President said: "I am no special friend of the Negroes, and if the necessity ever arises I will show you that I am not. I do not believe that the colored people should have special favors because they are colored, nor on the other hand, should they have special burdens because of their color.

"America is a great Darwinian field, dedicated by fate to the cause of genuine democracy, the rule of the united judgment of men. Here we are to have the wild, grand play of universally and absolutely unfettered forces, and out of the strenuous struggling the fittest are to survive, and the final man is to be evolved. I believe simply in giving the colored man the same chance in this great Darwinian field that other men are given, no more, no less. Now what have you to say to that?"

"Absolutely nothing, Mr. President," said Molair. "So far as I am concerned I ask nothing for me and mine that I begrudge to the colored man. What I have come to ask of you is along another line. Your party, I fear, has sometimes been a little insincere in some of its utterances, has made declarations for political effect, simply. Hereafter confine your party utterances to just such things as you really mean to do. For heaven's sake don't make our race question a political football. The issues are too grave.

"Inflame the masses of the South by meaningless baits to the Negro voter if you choose, but remember that this course vitally affects the welfare of the race concerning which interest is professed. For out of this inflamed mass we have to draw policemen, constables, sheriffs, legislators and juries. If we of the South can just get rid of that part of the entanglement which is only political by-play, the insincere part of the programme, not much trouble will be caused by what your earnest, high-minded men and women have to advise."

In great detail Molair now went into the Southern situation and cited move after move, the insincerity of which was subsequently demonstrated, but which was in the public eye long enough to do great harm to the South and the Negro.

The showing made a marked impression on the President, who now said:

"I regard your request, Mr. Molair, as a reasonable one and I pledge you my support in trying to have my party deal sacredly with this question; say nothing but what it means. Now, Mr. Molair, will you agree to do as much in the South? In cases where there has been absolutely no cause to fear the Negro a hue and cry of Negro domination has often been raised by men in your section. Cannot both sections rise to the plane where we will not make a football out of this helpless, unarmed race, Mr. Molair?"

"Yes, yes, I will do all that I can," responded Molair, aware of the great task before him.

The interview now came to a close and as Molair left the White House he said to himself, "When political by-play is eliminated North and South much that produces pessimistic Letitia Gilbreaths will then disappear. With the President working to that end in the North and the house of Molair committed to that policy in the South, who will say that we shall not win?"

CHAPTER XXIX.

MOLAIR AND AN OLD FRIEND.

FROM Washington, Molair now journeyed to the city of New York in quest of a former Belrose boy, a boon companion of his younger days, who had plunged into the commercial life of the great metropolis and won for himself the title of multi-millionaire. As Molair drew near the magnificent Fifth Avenue mansion of this former Belrose boy, Herbert Rogan, he paused for a moment's meditation.

"Yes, I'll go. It is not for myself. I know Herbert's heart is yet warm with love for the South. We never forget," said Molair.

Reaching Rogan's home Molair was admitted by a servant and escorted to the waiting room. While sitting here his eye quietly wandered around the room noting the evidences of great wealth everywhere abundant.

"Why hello, Seth! If you were only the hundredth part of a lady I would kiss you, I am *so* glad to see you, boy," said Rogan with great cordiality.

"No more glad to see me than I am to see you, Herbert," said Molair soberly but feelingly.

The genuine warmth of the greeting of his boyhood friend who had become one of the world's richest men deeply touched Molair, for he had somewhat feared that great riches might have, to some degree, affected the warm, open Southern heart of Herbert.

The two now retired to Herbert's private den where they could engage in a heart-to-heart.

"Well, Rogan," began Molair, "I disagreed radically with your course in coming north hunting for the golden fleece, but you came and now here I am at your feet."

"No, no, Molair, it is I who am at your feet. How often have I recalled your words to me, urging me to not enter the mad, mad, American race for wealth. I did not heed your voice and have gained my millions. I hope that I escaped the drain on my soul which you feared, and if I have I owe it to the exhortation that you gave me to take care of the Herbert that was within me. So, I say I am at your feet."

"I am so glad that the warm-hearted, patriotic Southern heart is not dead in you, Herbert, for just now we have need of you," said Molair.

A mere suggestion that the South needed him was sufficient at any time to quicken Rogan's interest, and he said, "Out with it, Seth. I am ready for the bugle blast at any moment."

"Now my mission is this, Herbert. We of the South have been cruel to our poor whites. In the days of slavery we kept them back by making use of slave labor. In those days there sprang up an animosity between the sleek, well-fed Negro slave and the poor whites who accused the Negroes of keeping them poor by working for nothing. This element of whites has been emancipated by the freer conditions of labor that came after the war, is fast finding itself and is marching to the front to take charge of affairs. It has discovered its power and is going to use it."

"You have sized the situation up exactly. It was partly because I saw the coming of this regime that I fled the South, Molair. I saw that our day was over, that the day of the common man was on in the South. But go on," interposed Rogan.

"Now there came over from slavery," resumed Molair, "the inherited feeling of the poor white toward the Negro, which feeling is accentuated by the fact that the Negro is yet his industrial rival. Here then is a veritable gold mine for the demagogue. In return for office he tosses to this element the Negro, hobbled, gagged or quartered according as he thinks will most please this element."

"A sad, sad situation," said Rogan.

"Now our hope is to free the South from that man whose chief stock in trade is hatred of a weak and despised class. We may not convert or deter the demagogue, but we can lift our people beyond his reach."

"A stupendous task, a long drawn out struggle," said Rogan.

"That is true, very true. The fact that in the South we have a double school system adds to the size of the problem of education. I have come to ask you, Herbert, to devote some of your millions to the education of our neglected white population."

Without indicating whether Molair's request met with favor or disfavor, Rogan arose and said: "Come with me to my office, Seth."

On the way to the office Rogan was silent. His mind was once more in Dixie. He was playing by the side of the babbling brooks, gathering daffodils from her fields, chasing lightning bugs in the gloaming, speeding over her country roads in buggies seated by the side of Dixie's fair daughters, listening to the plantation melodies of the Negroes surging from their warm, emotional hearts. Turning his head from Molair he dashed away a tear.

When the men entered the office, Rogan opened his safe, took out his books, and recounted his holdings to Molair, demonstrating to him that he was far wealthier than what the outside world estimated.

Finally Rogan said: "Now, there is my fortune, Molair. I say to you in all sincerity that I stand ready as far as is within my power to respond to any call that you may make. Our poor, struggling section, with the most complicated problem of all of human history must have culture, must have culture."

Molair was deeply touched by the confidence in his consideration and judgment shown by the most unusual offer of Herbert, and it was with difficulty that he could keep back the tears.

"Now Seth, since that point is settled, there is a matter in which I am interested to which I would like to call your attention," said Rogan.

"Say on Herbert, I do hope that I can help you."

"I have watched with great interest your recent efforts to bring political peace between the white and colored people of the South. I hope that you will succeed. The war of spirits in the South is fast affecting the whole country. It is bringing to the North hundreds of thousands of Negroes utterly unprepared for Northern life, and the suffering among them is something fierce. In some sections they have aroused a hostility far more intense than anything we have in the South. So the coming of the unprepared is bad for themselves and bad for their race.

"Moreover, politicians hostile to the economic needs of the South, use these Negroes to make politically hostile states that could at one time be relied upon to now and then join hands with the South. If you will study the distribution of the colored population and take into account the normal alignment of white voters it will be apparent that the colored people can in normal times practically veto all of the South's national aspirations, and absolutely forbid policies suitable to the economic needs of the South. In close elections they are the balance of power. From our viewpoint this is an unpleasant fact, but it is nevertheless a fact. Now the Negro is naturally a home lover, a patriot. If you can honorably do so, make terms with him in the South and word will come northward that will break up this solid mass of hostility to the South," said Rogan.

"Yes, yes, another serious complication, but in Belrose we have learned to get together and before many years you may expect to find the colored people working enthusiastically for a Southern man for President," said Molair.

Now that political and philanthropic forces gave promise of turning their faces in the right direction so far as the South was concerned, Molair returned to Belrose feeling assured that the outlook was bright for the killing of the destructive germs to be found in minds on the order of that of Miss Letitia.

But as we shall now shortly see fate had a far different way of curing Miss Letitia's pessimism.

CHAPTER XXX.

THE RUDOLF FIRE.

ONE evening about the set of sun, the city of Belrose was aroused by the ringing of the central fire bell. The people of the city, wherever they chanced to be, paused to count the strokes of the gong, that they might, with the aid of the signal, consult their charts and thus locate the fire.

"Near Rudolf's!" Such was the startling piece of information that passed from lip to lip.

Rudolf's was by all odds the finest store in the city, and perhaps the finest in the South. As for Mr. Rudolf himself, he was a man of genial personality, a patriotic citizen, anxious for the city's growth, and he possessed in a marked degree the spirit of philanthropy. As a consequence he had won the esteem and affection of the entire population of Belrose, without regard to class or race.

So, when it was noised abroad that the fire was near Rudolf's, great anxiety was created, and there was a universal rush for the scene of the conflagration.

The first engine to arrive on the scene was that of the colored company.

The building which was on fire was not Rudolf's but the one across the alley from it.

The firemen went gallantly to work to combat the flames, but the fire continued to make rapid headway. Like so many great hungry tongues, the flames leapt out of the windows of the burning structure and seemed to knowingly lick at the Rudolf building across the way.

As Conroe stood looking at the menacing, raging flames, many thoughts came surging to his mind.

"All Belrose is out to-night, and all Belrose will talk of what is done here. The South knows of our fathers, knows how that in peace and war they followed the call of duty. We can this night demonstrate that we are the sons of our fathers," reflected Conroe.

"The only way to save the Rudolf is to mount its walls and fight the flames from the roof, but that is a great risk," thought Conroe.

Further and further out reached the tongues of fire, their failure to reach the Rudolf seeming to enrage them, and each effort appeared to be more strenuous than its predecessor.

"The Rudolf is doomed," was the thought in the minds of all.

"A ladder! a ladder!" shouted Conroe. A ladder was brought and placed beside the wall of the Rudolf. Conroe put one foot and a hand on the ladder, turned to his comrades and shouted: "Men, there is danger on this wall. I will not order you to go, but who will volunteer to follow me?"

Two men hurried to his side and, amid the cheers of thousands, they ascended the ladder and ranged themselves on the wall.

Of course Miss Letitia was there, for when had she missed a fire since there had been colored firemen?

"My, ain't that grand! Ain't that inspiring! Now, ain't that grand!" Such were the exclamations arising from Miss Letitia, as, with hat thrown back on her head, her face wearing a rapt expression, she gazed upon the three men fighting the flames. When gusts of smoke would engulf the men she would stand with clenched fists, the picture of distress, but when they again stood out in bold relief in the glare of the flames, she would heave a sigh of relief.

"Look out! Look out! Look out!" "Down! Come down!"

Such were the cries that came like a mighty roar from the throats of thousands of people who had seen the wall of the burning building spring and get ready for a fall. The men on the wall of the Rudolf did not comprehend the meaning of the shout, so kept on fighting the flames.

"Down! Come down!" the multitude continued to shout.

Miss Letitia had seen the danger and had madly struggled through the crowd until she reached the ladder planted against the wall.

"Dont, woman! For God's sake, don't!" shouted the throng, while one man put a restraining hand upon her shoulder.

"Let me alone! I'll not let these brave fellows die," said Miss Letitia, springing up the ladder with the agility of a lad.

Mounting the roof, Miss Letitia screamed, "Men, come down. The wall is about to fall!" Seeing that they heard her, Miss Letitia turned and began the descent.

The men made a rush toward the ladder, but it was too late. Full against the Rudolf the wall of the burning building came with mighty force.

A roar of horror arose from the throats of the assembled thousands, but Miss Letitia and the firemen who had gone with the wall heard it not.

Their ears had become attuned to the music or the noises of another world.

CHAPTER XXXI.

A FORTUNE SPURNED.

"I HAVE sinned! I have sinned!"

With the tears pouring down her cheeks, and her frame shaking with the emotions that swept through her being with cyclonic force, Clotille stood thus addressing Baug, who had called to express his profound sorrow over the loss of his friend and her husband, Conroe.

"Bear up; be brave," said Baug, comfortingly.

"How can I, Baug, when Conroe is dead, and I must bear the responsibility of his death?"

"Clotille, you are in no wise responsible for Conroe's sad end. He died a death that any one might well envy—died in the line of duty."

"Ah! but you don't know, Baug! Baug, this commercial age sent a part of its atmosphere into my heart. I thought too much of a fortune. When I found it standing between me and Conroe I should have spurned it at once; should never have dallied with it. I always meant to spurn it if it sought finally to block our pathway, but I waited too long, too long."

Clotille sobbed so violently that she had to pause.

Resuming, she said: "The fact that I dallied with this fortune, allowed it to postpone my acceptance of Conroe, caused him to feel that I greatly desired it. It was largely in the hope of softening Cousin Letitia's heart that he gave up his profession and entered the fire department, and now—now—poor Conroe is dead—dead—and shall never more open his lips to cheer my heart with a message of love."

"Take a seat," said Baug, leading Clotille to a chair.

When she was more composed she said: "It has been discovered that Cousin Letitia did not carry out her purpose to disinherit me. An unfinished will which she was trying to draw herself was found by the side of the one which she had made in my favor but was planning to alter. So her death has brought me her fortune."

Clotille lifted her eyes to Baug's face and said: "If anyone had told me two days ago that I could despise money, I would have denied it. But today I despise it! I despise it with all my heart. Before God, I shall never touch a penny of my cousin's money for myself. It is blood money! It is blood money!" Clotille now broke forth into weeping afresh, followed by a long period of silence. At last she said:

"Come, Baug, let us look at him."

The two now entered the room where Conroe's body lay in a coffin ready for its journey to its narrow home. Baug looked down upon the face of his friend so serene in death, and murmured: "Happy boy; free at last."

"Baug, in this sacred presence, I want you to

promise me that you will take one-half of this money that will come to me and use it to help bring to the colored man a man's chance as a colored man. I want to see to it that no other dark couple has the struggle that Conroe and I had.

"I shall not use the other half, but why I retain it will appear later. Will you do this for me? It will be something of an atonement for my sin," said Clotille, softly, sadly, earnestly.

Baug extended his hand across the bier to grasp the outstretched hand of Clotille, and the two looked into the face of Conroe, who seemed to smile his assent.

Baug said: "Clotille, I will do as you say and will consecrate the fund to the lifting of the shadow."

CHAPTER XXXII.

A BADLY NEEDED OPENING.

IN a corner of the part of the Belrose depot designated for the use of colored patrons, Uncle Jack and Baug sat awaiting the coming of the train that was to bear the former to the state of Alabama for the purpose of inaugurating a test of the clause of the recently adopted state constitution that provided for the elimination of the illiterate Negro voter without affecting to the same degree the illiterate white voter.

"I would not have you think, Uncle Jack, that I am using you for a personal service, purely. It is true that the pressing of this case will in all likelihood bring me once more under the same roof with Eina under circumstances that will permit my speaking to her without inviting mob violence, but beyond that, what we are doing is in keeping with a vital need of the hour.

"It is often asserted, Uncle Jack, that our rights came to us amid the lingering passions of war and should not be taken as the sober sense of the American people. If we can get an authoritative expression from our highest court in this sober day of peace, it will count for so much," said Baug.

"Uv co'se I doan' 'zackly understan' de full uv de high falutin' pints yer make, Baug, but I hez my idees on de qusshun. I ain't goin' into dis heah testin' businiss jes' ter bring yer an' Miss Eina nigh ter each udder, while dat is part uv whut I am atter. But I hez had time ter thort out dis thing, an' heah is my thorts.

"Dey says dat Abe Linktum said dat Ameriky coulden' be kep' part one thing an' part er nudder, an' I sees dat dis whole country is one day goin' ter drink outen one spoon 'bout de cullud man. Ez er cullud man it is my lookout ter see ef dis one spoon is ter be er brass spoon er er silvah one.

"Den ergin er ill littered white man is my or-rival. I got ter work wid him, got ter go ter law wid him, an' sometimes got ter sass an' ter fight wid him, perhaps. Now ef yer let er ill littered white man vote, an' doan' let me vote yer give him dat much ekvantage uv me. Now I doan' want er ekvantage uv nobotty, but in jestice ter myself I doan' want nobotty ter git er ekvantage uv me."

"Well, Uncle Jack, I am glad that you see in your way the deep issues involved. Of course, I don't know just what your plan is, as it was Miss Rapona's desire that I not know, but I am sure that she consulted some eminent authority before she advised you as to the course to pursue. All I have to say to you, Uncle Jack, is that I love you as dearly as I ever could have loved a father had I known one, and I want no harm to come to you. Be careful of yourself."

The tremor in Baug's voice warned Uncle Jack that the conversation was taking too serious a turn, so he decided to have a hearty laugh in an effort to cheer somewhat Baug's spirit.

"Doan' be uneasy, Baug. I knows de white people putty well, an' knows how ter not git in too tight er fix," said Uncle Jack.

"I hope so, certainly, Uncle Jack. I crave to have these laws overthrown, I crave to see Eina, but I want dear old Uncle Jack to live, too," said Baug feelingly.

"Speakin' uv tight fixes 'minds me uv er time wunst w'en I wuz er gardenin' fur a white fambly," began Uncle Jack, determined to have a last laugh with Baug before they separated. "My room wuz out in de yard an' de cook staid in de main house ovah de dinin' room. Wal, hard times kinder struck de country an' throwed er lot er men out uv wuk. Dis heah cook wuz er good gal, all right, but she pinched off er leetul ter help her beau keep frum gittin' hungry durin' uv de hard times. Dis beau had er way uv creepin' ter dis gal's room jes' fo' breakfas' an' havin' her bring him up sumpin' ter eat.

"Wal, one mornin' he wuz up stairs eatin' erway, an' his eatin's run out fo' he wuz through. He heered some one walkin' in de dinin' room under him, an' he thort it wuz de cook, but it wuz de white lady. He says, says he, 'Honey, bring me up ernudder cup uv coffee an' ernudder hot biscuit." De white 'oman stopped ter listen, an' de feller thinkin' dat de cook didunt quite heah said er leetul louder, 'Say, honey, bring me up er nudder cup uv coffee an' er nudder one uv dem white folkses nice warm biscuits.'

"De white 'oman went back an' tol' her husban' whut she heered."

"Hah! hah! hah!" laughed Uncle Jack. "It makes me laf ter think erbout it," said he.

"Wal, de white man got er good cow hide an' creeped up de stairs atter dis cullud feller. Kaint yer 'magine how his eyes bucked w'en dat white man come in dat room an' seed him eatin' his grub? De cullud feller managed by skummishin' 'roun' to git 'tween de white man an' de door, an' down de stairs he run, de white man right atter him.

"De cullud feller thort he would run right outen de back gate, but it wuz shet. So he kep' right on 'roun' de hous', hopin' ter gain ernough distance ter git time ter open de gate w'en he passed de nex' time. But w'en he retched de gate de secon' time, de white man wuz still pushin' him mighty close.

"By dis time de noise 'tracted me, an' I come out ter see whut wuz de mattah. Ez I wuz standin' dare lookin' heah comes de cullud feller fur de third time, runnin' an' puffin' an' blowin', an' de white man right atter him, cuttin' at him wid de cow hide fur ev'ry step he wuz takin'.

"As de cullud man swep' by me lak er lightin' 'spress he shouted back, 'Say, mistah gardener, please sah, if yer please, please sah, hab dat gate wide open by de time I gits dare on my nex' roun'.'

When the laugh that followed the anecdote was over, Uncle Jack added: "Yer see, Baug, I understan's de white people, an' I'll try ter have de gate open whenevah I sets down ter eat grub dat dey doan' want me ter eat."

At length the Alabama train was called out, and Uncle Jack was escorted by Baug to the gate leading to the train. A hearty hand shake, a steady looking into each other's eyes, and Uncle Jack was off. Peace be to his good intentions whatever may betide his bones.

CHAPTER XXXIII.

SUNSHINE AND STORM.

AS was its wont, the election at the Oak Cliff precinct, a few miles out from the city of Birmingham, Ala., was proceeding orderly, the voters arriving, depositing their ballots and quietly returning to their several homes. An hour or so before the time for the polls to close, Uncle Jack, who had taken up his residence in that State and section, came sauntering up to the door of the small store-room in which the election was being held.

The all-day watching on the part of the election officials of the depositing of ballots in an unexciting election had been a rather tedious affair, and as they caught sight of Uncle Jack a smile of pleasant anticipation appeared upon their faces. They thought to beguile away the time with a few anecdotes from Uncle Jack, who during his residence there had from time to time enlivened groups of white and colored men with his humorous stories to such an extent as to establish his reputation as an entertainer.

"Come in, Uncle Jack, come in," said the election judge sitting immediately behind the table on which stood the ballot box.

Uncle Jack did as bidden, and took a seat that was proffered him.

"Say, old fellow, tell us something," said the election judge who had extended the invitation, tilting back his chair, a merry twinkle in his eye. The other election officials joined in the request, and Uncle Jack yielded to the demand.

"It is er great wonder ter me how times do change. Frum whut I kin fin' out dey now got yer white folks doin' whut yer all once had us doin'," began Uncle Jack. Judging that this was a precursor of some humorous incident, Uncle Jack was asked encouragingly to explain himself.

"Sometimes er man wants ter do whut he thinks is right, but on ercount uv some one else he doos whut he doos, an' then hez ter tell er fib erbout it. Now, yer white folks is goin' ter want dis heah 'lection to 'pear ter be in keepin' wid de United States Constertution w'en it ain't."

"What on earth is there funny about that, Uncle? We are looking to you for a joke, not a lecture on constitutional law," said the judge.

"I is gittin' down ter de joke part. Yer see I coulden' help frum thinkin' how yer all hez ter scramble 'roun' an' stretch de trufe er leetul lak we use ter have ter do. Dey say it made us bad an' sneaky. Ef it did, I hopes it won't do de same fur yer all."

"Now you are lecturing us on morals. Get down to the joke."

"All right den. Speakin' 'bout how er man hez ter some times scramble ter git outen er thing 'min's me uv ole Joe, whut use ter b'long ter my ole massa. Ole Joe jes' would steal hogs. He would say dat his labor fed de hogs, an' dat his stomick wuz jes' kerlectin' honis' debts whut ole massa failed ter pay. His stomick wuz er shuah 'nough good kerlecter, too.

"Wal, ole massa kinder caught on ter ole Joe an' one night er short while atter he heered er pig squeal, he started towards ole Joe's cabin. Ole Joe had spies out whut whistled er long ways off ter let him know dat massa wuz comin'. Quick ez er flash ole Joe grabbed his leetul baby gal dat wuz in de cradle, handed it ter his ole 'oman, an' sent her runnin' out uv de cabin wid it. Ole Joe den took de pig, slapped him in de cradle, kivered him up, an' swep' de scraped off hair uv de pig back in er corner uv de room.

"W'en massa come in de cabin ole Joe wuz sittin' down by de cradle jes' ez meek ez er lamb, rockin' it an' singin'

> " 'Rock er bye baby in de tree top,
> W'en de win' blows der cradle will rock;
> W'en de tree breaks de cradle 'ull fall,
> An' down 'ull come baby an' cradle an' all.'

" 'Whut is de mattah dare?' axed massa.

" 'My baby is mighty sick, mighty sick, massa,' said ole Joe.

" 'Dat's too bad. Lemme take er look at her,' said massa.

"Ole Joe's eyes bucked wide, he wuz so skeert.

" 'Naw, naw, massa; Granny White says dat ef

de air straks dis baby gal er mine it'll shuah kill it, shuah kill it, massa, shuah kill it.

" 'I'll not keep de kiver up long, Joe. I jes' wants ter see how de baby looks. A leetul air mout he'p de baby,' said massa.

" 'Now, massa, Granny White pintedly says dat jes' one breaf uv air will kill de pore thing. I been kinder feered ter breathe fur fear er gust uv breaf mout reach de leetul one an' kill it,' said Joe, makin' out he wuz 'bout ter cry and pattin' de pig right sof' an' tender lak an' tryin' ter look ez ef his heart wuz erbout ter break.

" 'Dat song yer wuz singin' wuz stirrin' up air,' said massa.

" 'Uv co'se, massa, yer kin out argify er pore slave lak me, but yer kaint keep me frum havin' er tender heart fur my young un,' whined ole Joe.

" 'Wal, I am jes' goin' ter look at dis baby, ennyhow,' said massa, walkin' towards de cradle.

"Ole Joe got up an' inched towards de door, saying, 'Wal, massa, yer is boss, an' whut yer says hez ter go. Ef yer jes' will kill my baby by lookin' at it, an' lettin' de air strak it, an' I jes' kaint 'suade yer ter not lif' de kiver frum it, I ain't got de heart ter stan' by ter see it die. So goodbye ter de baby an' goodbye ter yer.' So sayin', ole Joe lit out an' fairly flew, fur he knowed dat de sick baby wuz one uv massa's fat shoat pigs wid his throat cut frum year to year.

"Now fur my pint. Dis 'lection box heah ain't no more got ballits in it 'cordin' ter de constertution dan dat cradle had er baby in it."

A hearty laugh followed Uncle Jack's joke.

"Come give me your hand, Uncle. That is a good one," said the man behind the election box. Uncle Jack approached the man as if to grasp the proffered hand, but when over the box dropped therein a ballot which he had all the while kept concealed, watching for an opportunity to cast it.

"What have you done? You are not a registered voter," angrily spoke the election judge, who had invited the hand shake.

"I will 'splain ter yer, sah," began Uncle Jack. "I is er ill-littered man an' my grandaddy wuz er slave. Dey wouldn't put my name on de reg-'stration books 'cause my grandaddy couldn't vote. Ez my grandaddy wuz kept frum votin' cause uv his color an' cause he wuz er slave, it is stretchin' color an' slavery down ter me terday fur me ter be shet out on 'count uv my grandaddy's short-comin's. Ter stretch color an' slav'ry lak dat is pintedly 'gainst de constertution uv de United States. Ez I wuz shet out uv de reg'stration by unfair means, I done come straight ter de 'lection."

"You have violated the law, sir, and you will be jailed," angrily shouted the election judge.

"Now dat is whut I am aimin' at. I done voted. I wants ter see ef de S'preme Coat will stan' fur me bein' punished fur not 'beyin' er law whut doan' itself 'bey de constertution."

"Take that, you scoundrel, trying to overthrow the law of the sovereign State of Alabama," said the election judge, shooting his fist with great force squarely into Uncle Jack's face.

The old man tottered back, then fell, his head striking the wall of the narrow room with great force. Being badly injured by the fall, Uncle Jack was rendered unconscious and could not rise. A wagon was summoned and the wounded man placed therein. He was rapidly conveyed to Birmingham, where he was turned over to the United States Marshal on the charge of illegal voting. Medical aid had been summoned as soon as Birmingham was reached, but an examination of the fracture of Uncle Jack's skull caused by the fall revealed the fact that he had but a short while to live.

The news of Uncle Jack's exploit reached the newspaper offices and a bevy of reporters, ever on the lookout for the fulfillment of that standing dream of a Negro uprising, rushed down to see him to get an interview, if possible, but Uncle Jack was found to be in no condition to be interviewed. He remained unconscious throughout the night, but on the morrow his mind became clearer.

Uncle Jack was apprised of the fact that he did not have long to live, and was asked whether he had any statement he desired to make. He signied his willingness to talk, and the reporters and jail officials gathered in his room in the hospital ward to hear his dying statement. His dark, sober face and whitened hair inspired a feeling of awe in those who gazed upon him as he sat propped up in bed.

Uncle Jack began: "All uv my days, gemmens, I hez been er cullud man dat tried ter git er long wid de white folks. I allus jes' nachally laked white folks. I laked de gran' way dey walked an' talked. I laked de way dey wern't skeert uv no botty. I laked 'um fur feelin' lak purtectin' de wimmin folks. Ter make er long story short I jes' nachally laked white folks.

"I didun't allus 'gree wid 'um, but I allus could sepurate dare civil acts frum dare pussonal ones. Pussonally dey wuz fur me. Civully dey wuz er gin me. We got er long cause w'en I met de pussonul man I could furgit fur de time bein' de civul man. Now, I hopes dat de white folks will sepurate me de same way. Whut I hez done ain't pussonul, but civul. Make dat ez plain ez de nose on yer faces, gemmens.

"Tell de white folks dat ez er slave I done my bes'. Tell 'um how I keered fur my missus an' her dorters in de war times. Tell 'um dat I nevah done er crimial ack in my life, an' dat I died tryin' ter keep frum bein' blamed fur whut my gran-daddy coulden't do, 'cause he wuz er slave. Tell 'um dat I died in jail. I wuz tryin' ter git my case ter de S'preme Coat uv de United States, but frum whut dey tells me my case is goin' even higher dan dat, goin' ter de S'preme Coat erbove." Uncle Jack paused awhile as if meditating. Resuming, he said: "I ain't sorry. I feels shuah dat I'll git jestice up dare. Yes, git jestice up dare."

Uncle Jack's eyes now closed, and seeing that his little strength was rapidly failing, he was laid down again. Ever and anon he would look from one face to another as if hunting for some look of sympathy, but those about his bedside all happened to be out of sympathy with his aspirations.

"Gemmen, could yer—let some cullud pusson come in? I'm lonesome," said Uncle Jack, feebly.

The jail cook, who was a colored man, was summoned, and when Uncle Jack caught sight of him with his white cap and apron and looked into his large dark face, he smiled contentedly.

The day had been cloudy, but the clouds now stepped from the face of the sun and its rays struggled through the iron bars to the floor near the foot of Uncle Jack's couch. With his eyes fastened on these few streams of light and a happy smile upon his face, Uncle Jack, at heart the friend of all men, breathed his last.

CHAPTER XXXIV.

A CHINESE LADY.

IME wore on. Days, weeks, months, and a few short years which seemed to Baug an eternity passed away.

In the chamber of the Supreme Court of the United States, on the morning set for the hearing of the suit brought according to plans mapped out by Baug to have declared null and void the clauses of the Constitution of a certain Southern State intended to grant to illiterate whites privileges denied to illiterate Negroes on the same general level, Baug Peppers sat in such a manner as to have a commanding view of each entrance and of the audience. He was on hand early, in fact, was the first to arrive, and was determined to thoroughly scrutinize the face of every woman to be seen in the court room that day, for he felt that here was his one last certain opportunity to find Eina Rapona.

As the hour for the hearing of the case drew near, the audience-room began to fill, and Baug was kept busy looking from face to face in the hope of beholding the one face. At length the room was filled, every seat being taken save one that had been reserved for the wife of the Chinese minister.

Baug's heart grew heavy. The question as to

whether the great American nation was to make good her grant of equality of citizenship to the race of darker hue was now to be argued by him, and he felt the need of being in the best possible mood to present the case. But, with no Eina present, the weight of ten thousand worlds seemed to be upon him.

Although Baug knew that the one vacant seat was for the wife of the Chinese minister, the fact that any seat was yet empty was a slight source of comfort, the drowning man's straw. Presently there was a rustling of silks down an aisle as a lady, clothed in the Chinese garb and thickly veiled, came straight to the one vacant seat. All hope now departed from Baug, and despair settled over his soul.

"Poor, poor millions in need of an advocate this day! Upon a broken reed, upon a lacerated heart, upon a crushed spirit, upon a dead man who yet breathes, your hope at this hour is made to depend. But, I will do my best! I will do my best!"

So reflected Baug as he sat awaiting the filing in of the Justices. At length the Justices marched in, walked to their respective seats, and the famous case was ready to be called. Baug now left his seat and took his place among the lawyers connected with the case.

Just behind where Baug had been sitting was Clotille, holding in her lap chubby little Conroe, who had entered the world shortly after his father's death. Baug had been in the direct line of vision between the lady with the Chinese garb and Clotille, so that this lady did not see Clotille and the boy until Baug arose to leave.

"She has fainted! She has fainted!" said a woman near the lady of the Chinese garb, and two or three neighboring women rushed to her assistance. In their efforts to resuscitate her, they lifted the veil from her face, and when Clotille, who had observed the lady faint, caught sight of the face thus revealed she uttered a slight scream and rushed across the room. It was the long lost Eina!

Eina was soon restored to consciousness, and insisting that there was no danger of a recurrence of the trouble, retained her seat.

"See my little boy yonder, Conroe, Jr.? That was all a mistake," whispered Clotille, who then returned to her seat, and with a mother's pride, stood her little boy in her lap so that Eina might see him.

All this while Baug had been busy conferring with the lawyers, and had not seen what was transpiring behind him. So absentminded was he that one of his associate attorneys said to another: "What a dullard. How can a race of people amount to anything so long as it commits the leadership to such stupid fellows as this?"

Baug, having been looking around all the morning, from force of habit, now took another last look at the audience. Eina's veil was now lifted, and as Baug caught sight of her beautiful face, of those eyes that had ever been with him night and day, he grew dizzy and clutched the railing near which he sat.

CHAPTER XXXV.

A FRIGHTENED JUSTICE.

EVERY vestige of despair now left Baug's face, the shadows lifted from his spirit, and with the wine of a great love stirring his heart, he felt that he could that day plead the cause of a hundred million people.

As Baug arose to speak, practically every person in the audience was inclined to turn to his neighbor and ask, "Who is that fellow? It seems as though I have seen him before."

One of the Justices turned pale, trembled violently from head to foot, and eyed Baug with every symptom of an overpowering fear. One lady remarked to Clotille, "That Justice with the very bald head seems afraid of that fellow. Wonder why? He doesn't look dangerous."

When Baug uttered his first words, this justice arose and in a voice quaking with fear, said: "For good and sufficient cause, and in the name of high heaven, I move the adjournment of this court for a few moments, to decide in private a momentous question of procedure."

The strange request and the very evident agitation of the Justice created a sensation in the court room. The motion was allowed by the court, and the Justices retired, the terror stricken Justice looking back eyeing Baug all the way as he passed out.

"Justice Morrow, we will hear from you," said the Chief Justice, addressing the frightened Justice.

"I wish to know, sir, if it is to be the policy of this court to permit men long since dead to practice before it. Are we going to recognize spiritualism to that extent?"

The Justices looked amazed.

"Explain yourself," said the Chief Justice.

"When I was a lad," said Justice Morrow, "a certain American statesman visited my home, played with me as a boy and gave me my first great impulse for the public service. He worked upon every fiber of my being, and his principles have shaped my innermost thoughts. He afterwards became ——— of our nation, and wrought well both in domestic and international affairs. His name is indellibly written in the life of the nation, his likeness adorns all our walls, his picture is in all of our school books. Show me the palatial residence—or the humble hovel for that matter, that lacks his likeness. Sirs, he died years ago, but he lives vividly in my mind, for he made me. Sirs," said Justice Morrow rising, "he is out yonder now, and though long dead, is opening this case this morning. He can't fool me. I see he calls himself Baug Peppers, but he is none other than ———."

It was thought best to humor Justice Morrow,

so Baug was summoned before the Justices for his satisfaction.

"Have I ever seen you before?" asked Justice Morrow of Baug, knitting his brow and directing toward him his most piercing look, taking pains however, to stand some distance away and put as many Justices as possible between himself and Baug.

"I do not know, sir. Practically every man I have met in my life has said that it seems as though he has seen me before, but I have yet to see one who could tell me when or where," said Baug.

"Who is your father?" asked Justice Morrow, putting a little greater distance between Baug and himself.

"I know not. He may have been hanged for aught I know," said Baug.

"Sir, you are the spirit of ———," said Justice Morrow, backing still farther away.

The Chief Justice took Baug in hand and said: "You say every one seems to have seen or met you before?"

"Yes," replied Baug.

"No one is able to state when or where?"

"Absolutely no one," said Baug.

"Gentlemen, I tell you I am right," interposed Justice Morrow now ready to leave the room entirely. "It is too uncanny. I like my Supreme Court duties but not well enough to hobnob with the dead," he said.

"By the way, I think I have the solution," said the Chief Justice. "Don't you recall, gentlemen, that ——— had a son who was the very image of his father and was disinherited. Evidently this colored man is an offspring of that boy. Because of this man's membership in the colored race, people have not thought to associate him with ———'s family. The universality of the impression is due to the wide circulation of ———'s likeness. ——— being white and having occupied the position that he did, the profound respect for the office has hitherto prevented the minds of the people from crossing over and making the comparison that would have explained all. It has been the case of a human puzzle picture. Trace that disinherited son, and I predict that you will find your journey's end in this man with the mysterious face."

Justice Morrow was somewhat mollified by this explanation, but decided to keep his eye on Baug just the same. The Justices now returned to the audience room and Baug resumed his speech. In that short conference another great shadow had been lifted from Baug's soul. He had found what he regarded as a clue to his parentage, a possible solution to the mystery of his face.

With that shadow lifted, and inspired by the presence of Eina, whom he hoped to meet after his speech was over, Baug made a plea of such power, that the opinion of the Chief Justice that ———'s blood coursed in his veins was fully confirmed.

In the course of Baug's pleading, one remark particularly had seemed to catch the fancy of the justices and the audience as well: "Sirs," said he, "if Anglo-Saxon blood lacks a champion on the other side of this case, let me for a moment step across the line and take up a cudgel in its defense. In its name I repudiate the thought of asking a handicap for the colored man in its race with him. I bring to you the message the true white Southernor would have me deliver: 'I want no laws of indulgence for me and mine. I spurn the thought of a lower test for Anglo-Saxon blood. If my son with a thousand years of civilization behind him cannot stand up in an equal fight with the great-grandson of a heathen and a savage, if he must be pampered and coddled with special laws, then I say with all my soul let him go to the wall.' "

CHAPTER XXXVI.

DISFRANCHISEMENT FORGOTTEN.

WHEN the argument in the great case was over and the Justices began to file out, scores in the audience pressed forward to grasp Baug's hand to congratulate him upon his effort. As that audience had listened to and had been swayed by his eloquence and the brilliance of his intellect it was the common thought that regardless of what the decision of the Supreme Court might or might not be, no human code could be made effective against the Baug Peppers type of men.

As for Baug, he could not show proper appreciation of the attentions being showered upon him at the conclusion of his speech for keeping his eyes on Eina, who neither came forward nor yet moved to go out. Now that she knew the truth with regard to Baug and Clotille, she did not care to share a hand shake with him with the rest of the throng, but desired him all to herself for a talk, and yet she was not conscious of one word that she had to say. She simply craved to be alone with him. Clotille, divining what was now to happen, was only too glad to hurry away so that she might no longer be in Baug and Eina's way.

Baug excused himself from his more enthusiastic admirers who had continued to remain behind, and got very busy arranging his papers. Soon the room was cleared of all save himself and Eina, and Baug now moved in her direction. Disfranchisement, Constitutions, Supreme Courts, the Belrose movement now all faded from Baug's mind as he once more stood in the presence of the queen of his heart.

"Are you ready to go, Miss Rapona?" asked Baug simply.

"Yes," said Eina, glancing up into Baug's face with such ineffable sweetness as to tax his power of self control to the utmost.

Eina was proud of the work Baug had done that day. The two walked out of the room and hailed a passing cab, into which they entered, and were whirled along toward the private residence where Eina had taken up her abode when she came to Washington to be in attendance upon the famous case. Neither Baug nor Eina for a time had one word to say. That larger vocabulary of sacred silence was now employed by these two hearts in their communing the one with the other.

At length feeling it incumbent upon him to say something Baug remarked: "Oh, that Uncle Jack might have been with us to-day."

"Why did you not bring him?" asked Eina.

"Poor, dear Uncle Jack is dead!"

"Dead! Uncle Jack dead! My dear heavenly father!" sobbed Eina, weeping bitterly.

It by no means improved her feelings when she found out that he died as the result of an effort to serve her cause. Baug, finding that Eina had kept herself absolutely out of touch with all that pertained to Belrose, now told of Conroe's heroic death, of the spread of the Belrose movement throughout the South, of the happy results that came from the harmonious co-operation of the better element of the two races, of Seth Molair's great popularity throughout the nation and the honors of a national character that evidently awaited him for having pointed the way for the peaceful adjustment of the race question in Belrose, which adjustment stood as a model of procedure for other communities. Eina heard with interest all that Baug had to say, but there was ever before her the kindly face of Uncle Jack.

At length they arrived at Eina's temporary home and she excused herself to dispense with her Chinese attire. When she reappeared she was wearing the dress that she had worn the last time prior to the break that she was in Baug's company, as much as to say to him, "Let us begin where we left off."

But Baug, who took the hint, was utterly unwilling for any such arrangement. As he recalled matters, at the time of the break he was daily trying to muster enough courage to enable him to reach the asking point, with a fair prospect of getting to that much desired state with a few more weeks of effort on his part and considerable more encouragement from Eina. But in the time of his enforced separation from Eina he had vowed before his maker that he would not return to this intermediate state, this sort of purgatory, but would at once make a straight dash for the heaven of his happiness, the securing of an acknowledgement from Eina that she loved him and would become his wife.

Baug arose to meet Eina as she entered and she read in his determined face his purpose to force an issue. Into Eina's beautiful eyes there came—whether she so willed it or not—a thrilling look of surrendering love that drove from Baug's mind as far too feeble the words with which he was to make known the state of his heart.

Glad, oh so glad, that her weary, aching heart so long exiled might now beat undisturbedly against Baug's great, strong breast, Eina yielded herself to his embrace.

"Eina, Eina," whispered Baug, "every atom of my soul loves you. Could you, do you, love me? Tell me that we shall evermore be one. Will you be my—wife?"

"There is nothing else for me to do, Baug. You have all the heart there is in me," said Eina, her beautiful embarrassed eyes scanning the floor.

Baug gently turned her face so that he might read in her eyes the full measure of her love.

And in the mutual gaze that followed, which

only genuine lovers can understand, all earthly troubles vanished.

* * * * * * * * * * *

When on national decoration days, loving hands are spreading flowers on the graves of the dead who perished during the Civil War, Clotille and Conroe Driscoll, Jr., Baug and Eina and little Clotille Peppers go forth to decorate the graves of Conroe and Uncle Jack, while Seth Molair forgets not to adorn with the most lovely flowers the grave of Aunt Lucy, who though a colored woman, lies buried in the plot of ground that holds the body of his father and awaits the coming of that of Molair's mother and himself.

In that one family plot, Southern at that, there is no color line.

THE END.